I0689189

The Mildly Inappropriate Space Ventures of WormBoy

Lisa Huff

I would like to thank my sister, Juliana Daniel, for editing this book and leaving all kinds of fun notes doodled all over the proof copy.

I also want to thank Christina Young for helping me get my book started.   www.getyourbookstarted.com

And finally, I'd like to thank all my friends who looked forward to my WormBoy short stories that I began writing to pass the time.

Please take the time to rate my book on-line.   I appreciate your feedback!

CHAPTER ONE

This, my friends, is the tragic tale of Wormboy (also known as Bleek.)

When Wormboy was born, his parents named him Jude. He had everything he needed and more, but when Jude was only twelve years old, his planet was destroyed by nuclear war over the course of two days.

Jude had been at school when the war began. The nearest nuclear bomb hit many miles away, but before death and destruction got close enough, an extraterrestrial took pity on his class and beamed them aboard his roomy vessel.

The alien from outer space let them live on his ship on the condition that he be allowed to experiment on them. Most of the class agreed. Several of Jude's classmates cried and begged to return home. The alien promptly fed them to his pet dinosaur.

Jude was not afraid of the alien and they quickly became friends. Jude named him "Spee," and Spee, who could not speak due to his superior anatomy, named Jude "Bleek", since that was the only noise he could seem to make with his nonexistent vocal chords.

Mrs. Farmer, the teacher of the abducted classroom, was frightened but smart enough to stay alive until, that is, she began concocting a plan of mutiny and escape. Spee's mind reading abilities picked up on Mrs. Farmer's mutinous thoughts so Spee decided that he would save the worst experiment for her; Spee permanently attached Mrs. Farmer to the the back of his purple pet T-Rex where its tiny arms could not reach her.

Mrs. Farmer tried to remove the attachments but was

harming herself and the dinosaur, so Spee removed her arms. Eventually, Mrs. Farmer bled to death, but only because she kept biting her tongue from bouncing up and down every time the dinosaur ran anywhere.

Spee conducted many experiments on the remaining students. Some of them lived and some of them died. A few of them just ceased to exist. Eventually, Spee ran out of students until the only one he had left was Bleek. Spee hesitated. Bleek was his favorite and he had grown quite fond of him.

Spee wondered why he hadn't saved one more child for his final experiment. He thought about returning to the planet to obtain another but the only life signs coming from the surface were weak. They would be tainted with radiation anyway. After much reluctance, Spee conducted his final experiment on Bleek.

Spee took comfort in his decision to leave the best experiment for last. He attempted to manipulate Bleek's DNA to allow him the ability to shape shift. The procedure was a complete success!!! Almost.

Bleek shifted into many different forms successfully but upon shifting back into his human form, his body would reject his wiener and it would fall off onto the floor. Bleek cried. It didn't hurt, but he could not understand how he was supposed to pee now.

Spee was horrified. He had ruined the breeding tool of his prime specimen! This must be fixed! Spee attempted many things to set things right but they all failed. He was ashamed of his failure. His home world would be devastated by it.

Spee was about to detonate his entire ship out of shame when he had one more idea. He wandered into the jungle habitat of his pet T-Rex on deck 89. There he obtained several worms from the soil. He remembered how amazing this creature was and how it
survived being severed into pieces.

After several attempts Spee was able to manipulate the worm into a prosthetic wiener and attach the little guy to Bleek's groin. Spee encouraged Bleek to shift. Bleek obeyed, shifted into a dog and then back into his human form. Upon returning to his natural form, his wiener again fell to floor.

Spee was about to detonate his roomy vessel in shame when suddenly something amazing happened! It grew back! Spee squealed with delight. Apparently, he had found a new sound to make besides the "bleeking." The new wiener was fully functional. It even looked real, mostly. The only side effect seemed to be its worm-like wiggles, as if it had a mind of its own.

Spee accepted this one flaw but made a mental note to work on it in the future. Bleek seemed to cheer up and Spee felt a sense of satisfaction.

And so began the adventures of Wormboy and his new friend Spee.

CHAPTER TWO

Bleek had woken from a nightmare. It was a scary one but he could not remember what happened. All he could remember was waking up running around his bedroom on Spee's roomy vessel as a turtle.

Bleek shifted back into his human form, waited for his wiener to grow back and set out to find his extraterrestrial companion. It took him several days but he finally found him on deck 47.

Spee rummaged around furiously through a pile of junk. He was on a mission. His prime specimen would soon be at optimal breeding capacity. Spee knew that if he were to be accepted back on his home planet, he must find a female companion for Bleek, but Spee could not find any planets nearby that contained human women.

Spee excitedly held up a small box he had found and began to tinker with it. As he was doing this, they picked up a distress call from a nearby ship. Spee dropped out of warp speed to investigate and opened a channel to converse.

Another alien, similar in appearance to Spee appeared on a large viewing screen. Bleek watched them exchange in a silent conversation. He giggled as the other alien motioned about animatedly. It flung its long skinny arms around as if it were running from a playground bully. When it heard Bleek giggling, it pushed its face against the screen as if to look closer at him. This made Bleek giggle even harder.

Spee looked at him disapprovingly and tossed him the box he had been working on. Bleek caught it and suddenly could hear their conversation!

The alien agreed to give Spee a couple of human girls they had abducted in exchange for a ship part that they needed.

Spee skipped about excitedly.

Bleek's eyes got really big and he shouted out, "Eeeeewwww! Girls have cooties!"

Spee had no record of this human disease but the other alien did not want to take any chances so he gave Spee all four of the human girls that he had. Spee was delighted but then Bleek took off running in fear of them.

Bleek's terror quickly melted when he remembered the pet T-Rex on deck 89. He was going to go play with it! Bleek ran to the jungle habitat control room and spent the rest of the day using a crane to pick up large chunks of meat that were grown in the meat lab and used them to tease the large purple dinosaur. This was hilarious to Bleek at first, but then he became bored and decided to name the dinosaur Barney, after his uncle, who always wore a purple sweater and had really short arms.

At that very moment Bleek got the wonderful idea to knit Barney a purple sweater. He would have to discuss that with Spee at a later date.

A Spee hologram suddenly appeared and commanded him to return to meet the new female visitors.

"No!" Bleek shouted defiantly. Then he shape shifted into a fly and proceeded to elude capture for two weeks.

CHAPTER THREE

Spee was very excited to see what would happen when he performed the shape shifting experiment on his new specimens. He herded the four girls into his lab. Three of them were still crying. The fourth just looked around in curiosity and randomly picked her nose. Spee found this odd but he continued with his experiments.

The first girl grew a purple mustache, shape shifted into a dust mite and was accidentally inhaled by the girl next to her. The dust mite then shifted into an elephant and things got rather messy, if you can imagine. Needless to say, Spee was out of two test subjects already.

The third girl would not stop sobbing. Can you blame her after what she had just witnessed? Spee hurried with this experiment because he just wanted that horrible wailing noise to stop. Eventually, she morphed into a T-Rex and was not able to shift back. Spee's experiment had failed again. All was not lost however, for he now had a mate for his pet T-Rex on deck 89.

Spee frowned at the fourth girl. There was something odd about her. She reached out, poked his belly and giggled. Spee stared back at her, puzzled. He decided to go about this experiment differently.

He called for Bleek and tossed the girl a translator box. As Bleek entered the lab and stared at his shoes, Spee explained to the girl that she was to become like Bleek in the near future and then they would make lots of babies.

The young girl's large brown eyes widened. She pointed at Bleek and yelled, "Yuck! That boy has cooties!"

Spee made a note in his log to study this human disease. He could not have this disease running rampant on his ship.

Spee then performed the experiment on her. Everything seemed to be going as planned. The girl had successfully morphed into ten different forms without any major issues. The only side effect seemed to be a spaghetti-like substance that shot out of her nose every time she shifted. The substance was analyzed and found to be DNA waste from her previous shifts.

Bleek was really excited to have a new friend just like him, even if it was a girl.

"What's your name?" Bleek asked her cautiously. He could not remember if it was possible to contract cooties from talking to a girl, or if you actually had to physically touch them.

"Ana Shuezancar," she told him shyly with a strange accent.

"Ana Shuwhat?" Bleek had trouble pronouncing her name, "I'm just gonna call you Shuey, k?"

Ana liked her new nickname and proceeded to skip down the corridor repeating her name in a silly, high-pitched voice, "Shuweeeeee!!"

"Spee, why did I understand Shuey? Is she from my planet?" Bleek asked him while fiddling with the translator box in his hands.

Spee analyzed the skipping girl with the ship computer as she set out to explore the ship. "No," he replied after analyzing both of their DNA.

"Then why do we understand each other?"

"Sometimes humans are moved to other planets for various reasons," Spee explained, "Sometimes for overpopulation, other times for repopulation. The language would move with them, although I'm sure it has evolved differently on each planet."

Bleek nodded at Spee and decided to go make sure that Shuey picked a room that was far enough away from his that he would not smell or hear her. *She probably sings all the time too*, he thought with disgust.

Spee was delighted. Everything was going as planned. He would return to his home planet with Wormboy and Wormgirl and they would have lots of babies and Spee would sell them as pets and he would be accepted once again.

What Spee did not realize was that Shuey was a lesbian, but I'm getting ahead of myself. We will find out more about that later.

CHAPTER FOUR

Spee was not feeling well. He was starting to believe that he had contracted this "Cooties." After a few days of Spee moping around, Bleek decided to call the space nurse, Keely.

Bleek and Shuey loved Keely. She was a humanoid female alien who was so pale that she blended in with the white walls of Spee's ship, and all you could see were her eyes and mouth. Not only did Bleek and Shuey find this hilariously funny, Keely also gave them lollipops every time she visited.

Keely had been visiting a lot lately. Spee's new female T-rex got herself knocked up and needed frequent checkups. Also, Spee had Barney, the male dinosaur, fixed because Spee was having trouble growing enough meat in the meat lab to support two dinosaurs.

Shuey had a brilliant idea to fix this. She suggested that Spee use a shrink ray gun and breed an army of tiny T-Rexes that could power his ship by running in hamster wheels. Bleek also thought this idea was brilliant but Spee found the second part of her solution to be highly illogical.

Keely beamed herself onto the ship, handed the two worm children lollipops and proceeded to poke and prod Spee with a myriad of torturous looking devices. She turned to Bleek and asked him something but neither of the worm children heard her. Instead they erupted in hysterical laughter and were rolling around on the floor because all they could see were a pair of eyes blinking and a mouth moving. Keely stuck her tongue out at them.

"Can you tell me what symptoms you are currently experiencing?" Keely asked as she removed a tablet from her bag and opened his patient file.

"I have," Spee paused for dramatic effect, "the cooties."

He put the back of his hand to his large forehead and sighed with self-pity.

"Cooties you say?" Keely glanced up from the tablet and raised her eyebrows. She ran a quick search through her medical database to confirm her suspicions. Keely knew how to handle this. "Nonsense! Only human children can contract the cooties. It's just allergies."

She handed Spee a small container of allergy medicine, "How are you paying me today?"

Spee reluctantly handed her the large tank of helium she had requested. Bleek and Shuey frowned. They would no longer be able to change their voices and sing to the Tom Jones CD they had found on deck 42 while rifling through large piles of so called junk.

"If you'd like, I can cure the children of their cooties before I go," Keely offered.

Spee hesitated. He was afraid of what her price would be.

"No charge, of course." Keely added, knowing that cooties was a made-up disease that existed only in the mind.

"Yes, please," Spee clapped excitedly.

Keely removed a strange device from her bag. The outside casing of the device was translucent, revealing the inner parts and glowing lights flashing from inside of it. She turned a blue dial on the device and pointed it at the children. A strange bubble popping noise emitted from the wand-like device and a green laser shot out, stunning the children.

Fortunately for Bleek and Shuey, this did not hurt, but they began to belch. Loudly. The belching became so loud and so long that Bleek and Shuey spoke long sentences in belches.

"Take… me… to… your… lea…der," Shuey belched at Spee, who just looked back at her with mild disgust.

Now it was Keely's turn to laugh. She liked them but she was glad to be going back to her own ship where there were no children. She patted Spee on the head and wished him luck with the two kids. She reassured him that once the burping stopped, they would be cootie-free forever.

As Keely beamed back to her ship, Spee wondered why every time he thought he was sick, the space nurse said it was allergies. He opened the bottle, grabbed a pill and swallowed it.

In the background Bleek and Shuey were belching in a duet, "It's… not… un…us…ual… to… be… loved… by… any…one…"

CHAPTER FIVE

Many centuries ago, Spee was created in a pod. His species was unable to reproduce so they obtained all the genetic materials they needed from life on other planets. All genetic materials were taken from various living entities, genetically modified, and then placed in a birthing pod.

Spee and his fellow brothers and sisters took only several days to grow into fully functioning adults. When they were released from their pods, they were quickly sent off to be trained for their assigned jobs. Spee was originally assigned to be a spy.

Spee went through months of training before they finally gave him his own ship to go off on missions. It was a small ship but Spee was excited anyway. For his first mission, he was sent to a planet to observe life and take notes but he was warned never to interfere. At first he was happy with this. But planet after planet, Spee became annoyed.

Planet 892114 was his 25th mission. The life on this planet resembled humanoids but they still had tails. This planet was run by females. The males were second-class citizens. They could not vote, own land or hold jobs. They stayed at home raising children, had to cover their faces and were often victims of sex trafficking.   Spee felt sorry for them, so he abducted a rather large group of the men and a few of the women and dropped them off on a distant planet. He told the men that they could change things if they wanted to.   It is not Spee's fault that they took revenge and reversed roles.

Planet 9033772 was his 32nd mission. The planet was overrun with criminals and there were no longer enough jails and resources to imprison them all. At first Spee was going to just shoot them all with his laser beam, but then he realized this might be seen as an act of war. Spee then remembered the shrink ray gun his ship was equipped with.

He spent the next 30 days rounding up the criminals and shrinking them down to dollhouse size. He then gave the planet leaders the blueprints for the shrink ray gun with instructions on how it could be reversed so that the prisoners could be returned to their normal size once their sentence was complete.

The planet was very grateful for his assistance. They were able to fit every single criminal on the entire planet into one prison and it only cost almost nothing to feed all of them.

To show him gratitude, they called him "God" and placed a statue of his likeness to be worshiped. This is when Spee developed a small god complex.

Planet 18399303 was his 46th mission, and by now his god complex had grown incredibly large. He felt unstoppable. All life on this planet offended him. They were just ugly.

He picked the two prettiest people he could find and genetically altered their DNA. While they were aboard his ship, he flooded the planet. When the waters receded, he told them to go forth and multiply.

By now, Spee's home planet was beginning to learn about all the things he was doing. They sent out a ship to detain him and bring him back home. When they found him he was on planet 111100011 with a bunch of slaves who were building him a fleet of ships.

Unfortunately for Spee, he was easily apprehended and transferred back to home planet where they reset his brain. The leaders of the planet decided that Spee was too smart and was retrained as a scientist.

Everything was great again, for a while, until he went back in time and somehow made it impossible for his own race to reproduce. Spee was ashamed when he found out what he had done, for he was the very reason that he was grown in a pod.

For this crime against his planet, Spee was sentenced to be banished and was told never to return. Now Spee travels the universes, searching for ways to win back favor with his people.

CHAPTER SIX

Spee was working on his latest invention when the enemy ship attacked. The invention was top secret. It was so top secret that I can't even give you clues as to what it was.

Yeah, I completely agree that the author of these stories should be privy to that information but Spee insisted that I have a big mouth and can't keep a secret to save my life. I am determined to prove him wrong. For example, I've never told anyone about Spee's lover Eep…oh crap. Forget I mentioned that.

Anyway, Bleek and Shuey were off playing in the hallway when the alert notifications began to bombard their ears. They both covered their ears and ran off to find Spee. When they located him, Spee was running around the bridge, flailing his arms and furiously pressing buttons on his screen. He looked up momentarily when they entered.

Bleek tried to tell him that their ear drums were about to pop, but he was in too much pain. Luckily, Spee could read their minds as the sirens were so loud that he would not have been able to hear them otherwise.

He handed Bleek a caulk gun and suggested they use it. Bleek filled his ears and passed the caulk gun to Shuey who proceeded to fill her ears and nose, and her belly button.

The ship shuddered violently as it was fired upon. Spee instantly recognized the weapon signature. It was a M.E.R.P torpedo and there was only one evil being in the entire universe that used such a weapon. It was his arch nemesis Captain Herp Derp whose favorite weapon had always <u>M</u>ade <u>E</u>veryone <u>R</u>emove <u>P</u>ants.

Luckily, Spee had stopped wearing pants after his last encounter with the infamous Captain Herp Derp. Shuey and

Bleek however, removed their pants against their will.

Shuey giggled at Bleek's mermaid underwear. Bleek stuck his tongue out at her in response. It was the only clean underwear that he could find on the last merchant planet they had visited that fit his growing body.

Captain Herp Derp appeared on the screen in front of them. His amazing hair was the only good looking thing about him. It was dark brown and piled on top of his head, and it slightly resembled a cartoonish pile of poop. It was a good-looking pile of poop, mind you, if there ever were such a thing. His face was distorted in a Picasso-like fashion.

As Captain Herp Derp began his request for surrender speech, Spee silenced the alarms and Bleek removed his caulk plugs so he could listen. Shuey followed suit but was slightly distracted when she removed the belly button plug to see that it came out in the perfect mold of an ice cream cone. Yum! She tried to eat it. She succeeded.

Captain Herp Derp started his speech, "Ladeeth and Gentlemen of the worthst thpathip I haf ever theen, thurrender or thuffer my wraf. Shhhhhhh."

Bleek was confused by the Captain's shushing because no one had said anything. But then he quickly realized, after a few more sentences, that Captain Herp Derp had Tourette's Syndrome which caused him to say "Shhhhh" after every other sentence. How distracting!

Good thing he's not a school teacher, Bleek thought to himself. *And why is it that he can't pronounce his s or sh's sounds except for when he makes that shushing noise?*

Spee threw his hands out in response to Bleek's thoughts as his translator box said, "I know! Right?"

"I gif you one hour to thurrender. Shhhhhh."

Spee took a moment to contemplate his next steps. He considered the many reasons why Captain Herp Derp might be doing this. Revenge was the most probable. Spee thought back to when this all started.

Do you remember the story I told you about the time that Spee visited planet 18399303 on his 46th mission? It was the planet that offended him because they were all ugly.

On that planet, Spee thought he had destroyed everyone but the two prettiest people, but apparently, another meddling species of alien got wind of Spee's plans. They took pity on the unfortunate looking inhabitants and went down and told some guy name Hoan to build a big boat.

They told Hoan to collect supplies and board the big boat with his family. They also gave him a DNA reconstructor as a gift along with a disk that had all the DNA configurations of every animal on the planet to restore at a later date. Well as it turns out, Hoan had a son named Herp Derp, and that is how this whole charade began.

Spee decided that Captain Herp Derp was bluffing. The last time they crossed paths, Captain Herp Derp had fired upon Spee's ship with his M.E.R.P. torpedo and everyone on Spee's ship took off their pants. This was rather humiliating for Spee, as his secret crush (and possibly his secret lover at the time but you didn't hear that from me) was on board and present.

Spee probably deserved this and more for what he had done but he wanted to have the last laugh, so he visited several nearby planets and proceeded to leave obscene crop circles everywhere. He also signed them all as Captain Herp Derp.

Anyway, Spee was sure that Herp Derp was bluffing and that there was nothing to worry about. When Captain Herp Derp came back to him and said his hour was up, Spee laughed at him and said, "Try me!"

Immediately, Captain Herp Derp broad-casted video footage of Keely, the Palien, sitting under some rather large UV lamps.

"I'm so sorry Spee! I didn't want to tell him anything, I swear!" she apologized and Spee knew she meant it. Paliens knew that UV rays meant almost instant agony and death.

Captain Herp Derp stepped back into view, cackling evilly, "Thee told me aaaaall about your thapethifting thpethimens, shhhhhhh! You haf one hour to hand them over or thee diethes!"

Spee was instantly filled with dread but Bleek had been watching everything and he sprang into action. He traveled back to his special stash where he had hidden all of the treasure that he had found while adventuring around Spee's ship with Shuey.

One day they decided to play a game they called Frogger. They had each taken turns between driving an old truck they had found and shifting into a frog. The last time they had played, Bleek had nearly hit Shuey with the truck. He had swerved, causing the truck to overturn and pallets of SPF 1000 had spilled out over the pretend road they had created.

Bleek found the bottles right where he had left them.

He went back to get Shuey and before Spee could protest, Bleek beamed himself and Shuey aboard Captain Herp Derp's ship. Bleek was amazed at how small it was. The worm children quickly shifted into giant kangaroos. Bleek filled his pouch with bottles of sun protection and they hopped down the corridor until they found Keely's room of captivity.

As they blasted through the door, Captain Herp Derp's eyes widened and he reached for the UV light dial. Spee watched in horror as the UV lights flashed on. The door locked as Keely began to scream.

Shuey grabbed the SPF 1000 out of Bleek's pouch, cut Keely free and dumped the lotion on her head and any visible patch of skin she could find. Keely began to spread the lotion all over her quickly reddening skin while Bleek and Shuey beat up on Captain Herp Derp in kangaroo kickboxing style.

Spee was sure to record everything.

As soon as Captain Herp Derp was sufficiently defeated, and trembling cowardly on the floor, Bleek and Shuey unlocked the door and helped Keely out of the room, as she had so much lotion on her face and in her eyes that she couldn't see where she was going. Then they headed off to find the transport room so that Spee could beam them out safely.

24

CHAPTER SEVEN

Back on the ship, Bleek and Shuey helped Keely get settled, while Spee decided what to do with Captain Herp Derp and his ship.

Spee considered all of his options but the only one he kept coming back to was to destroy the ship with Captain Herp Derp on it.   He had a feeling that his arch enemy would never stop until he was dead.

Spee's ship suddenly notified him that Captain Herp Derp had turned on the warp speed engines and was preparing to escape.   With little time left to consider more options, Spee armed his main weapon and promptly fired.

The weapon's green laser directly hit the enemy's ship just as it has entered its warp jump. Spee shook his head and pounded his fist on the panel in front of him. The lights on the panels came on and a series of beeps and chirps bombarded Bleek's ears as he entered the room.

Spee looked angrily at Bleek.

"Why are you looking at me like that?" Bleek questioned him.

"Since when are you able to operate the beaming device on my ship?" the translator box yelled at Bleek.

Bleek did not answer. He debated whether or not to lie or tell the truth but he did not have to do either because Shuey showed up behind him. "It was me, Spee."

Spee's eyes grew wide with surprise.

"What would you know about beaming technology?" he asked her.

Shuey hesitated, because she was hiding a secret. It was a special secret that not even her best friend Bleek knew.

"Sometimes I just know things," she lied, "I was born on a

ship so I've been around technology since I was a small child."

Bleek noticed that Shuey was nervously looking at her feet and drawing random invisible things on the floor with her right sneaker.   He somehow knew she was lying, but he did not say anything because she was the one who had taught him how to use the beaming program.

Just then Shuey happened to notice a strange piece of paper sticking out of Bleek's back pocket. She saw strange pictures and lettering on it. Seeing a chance to change the subject, she grabbed the paper and unfolded it carefully.

Something else dropped from the folded papers and Bleek reached down to pick it up. He immediately started laughing. It was a photo strip of Captain Herp Derp in a photo booth and he had molded his poopy hair into different styles for each one.

Bleek showed it to Shuey and Spee. Shuey cracked up and even Spee let out strange chuckle. Spee's attention turned back to the unfolded papers that Shuey was holding and gasped.

As Spee grabbed the papers from her, a sun-burned Keely curiously entered the room. She no longer blended into the white walls of Spee's ship and this caused Shuey to make a sad face at Bleek.

"What are those?" Keely asked Spee, pointing to the papers he had laid out on a table nearby.

Spee gently rubbed his chin in thought, "It looks like a device that allows you to travel between alternate realities," he finally responded.

Keely looked at him puzzled, "What would you use that for?"

Bleek's mind was already considering the millions of possibilities the device could be used for.

"Does it have a name?" Shuey asked, "If not, I call dibs on naming it."

"It does not matter what it's called.   We don't need these blueprints because we're not building one," Spee announced to the group.

"Why not?" Bleek asked softly.

"Because of these," Spee pointed to a few pictures near the bottom, "These materials would be nearly impossible to obtain. I'm just wondering what Captain Herp Derp was planning on building it for."

Bleek immediately thought of a really good reason to build the device.

He had read a book once about alternate realities. The book talked about how there was a different reality for every decision you could have made at every possible moment, which means there are infinite realities.   There has to be a reality in which his planet was not destroyed by nuclear war and he might be able to return home. Bleek became very excited about this possibility, but how would he get Spee on board? And then it hits him.

"Do you think there is an alternate reality in which you were never exiled from your planet, Spee?" Bleek asked trying to sound like he was not up to something.

Spee considered his question for a moment.

"I suppose there would be quite a few realities where I had made different decisions that would not have led to me being exiled," he finally responded.

"Wait for it…" Shuey whispered, realizing what Bleek was up to. She picked up a desk lamp nearby, held it over Spee's head and turned it on.

It was almost as if Shuey's light bulb joke helped him because Spee suddenly got it.

"Bleek, that's a genius idea!" Spee began excitedly, "Perhaps we can find an alternate reality to move to where I can go home, and my people will practically worship me when they see my most successful experiment!"

"Or," Bleek chimed in, "We could also find realities for

Shuey and me to return to our homes."

Spee was not listening to him anymore.   Instead he was searching through his database looking for the locations of the three rare materials and parts they would need.

The first material was located on a water planet. Spee had heard of this planet. There were many stories about it. Ships were always going down or disappearing on it without a trace. It was dangerous, but Spee was feeling optimistic.

Spee continued searching for the other parts in the database. He groaned out loud when he discovered that two of the parts were probably being stored at one of Captain Herp Derp's "secret" labs. He knew that particular mission would probably be full of annoying obstacles, but Spee was confident in its success.

Spee moved on to research the final material. It was a special metal only found on Planet 85462M. Spee's already wide eyes became even wider.

"This mission is impossible.   We cannot complete it," he said and turned off the screen.

Keely happened to see the planet name before he shut it down.

"Isn't that a mining planet?" she asked with a mischievous grin.

Spee tried to change the subject but Keely would not let it go.

"I know who runs the mining operations on that planet!" Keely announced.

Bleek and Shuey looked at Spee and waited for him to answer.

"I can't go to that planet. It belongs to my home world. They would never let me land there," Spee explained.

"Aaaaand?" Keely tried to pry more information from Spee but when he would not continue she finished for him, "Spee's afraid to go there because his ex-lover runs the place and he's embarrassed about what happened between them."

Even though Spee did not usually utilize his mouth to speak, it was hanging open in disbelief.

"Nuh uh!" Spee tried to deny it.

Bleek grinned at Keely and tried to pry even more information, "Ooooo, what's her name?"

"Eep!" Keely could not hold it in.

"What's wrong?" Shuey asked Keely, thinking she was suddenly frightened by something.

"No, Spee's lover's name is Eep!" Keely punched Spee's shoulder, then remembered that it was actually how Spee's people challenge a ship captain for control of their ship.

Luckily, this was not the first time it had happened and Spee just rubbed his shoulder and glared at her.

"What happened Spee? Why don't you want to see her?" Bleek asked patiently, "Maybe it would be good to see her again now."

Spee sighed with his mouth.

"Everyone thinks it was because Captain Herp Derp shot the ship with his M.E.R.P. weapon and she saw me without pants, but everyone took their pants off. And most of my people don't wear pants anymore. After we survived that encounter with Captain Herp Derp, we were heroes and it became the new style."

Spee took a moment to gather his courage before finishing.

"The real reason I was embarrassed is because I had foolishly gotten a tattoo on my butt that said 'I love Eep' and that was before I had even told her to her face. She saw it and wouldn't talk to me. She avoided me the entire trip home then got reassigned to the mining planet. I haven't seen her since."

Spee looked very sad.

Shuey felt like she could almost relate to him in a way. She thought about all the times she had told a girl she liked that she loved her only to find out she liked boys and this was very confusing to her.

She remembered going home from school one day and asking her mom how she could tell if a girl likes girls or boys. Her mom answered, "Well dear, perhaps they would act and look kind of like a boy?" but this confused Shuey even further.   Why would she like a girl who looks and acts like a boy if she does not like boys?

Spee looked at Shuey curiously, as if he had picked up on the thoughts going on in her head, but luckily, he was too busy worried about seeing Eep and wondering why Shuey was always hiding small objects inside her belly button. Shuey was slightly concerned that Spee might pick up on her secret with his mind reading abilities so she moved her focus back to the missions.

"I'll help you, Spee," Shuey offered, "I can pretend I'm the captain of this roomy vessel and we can see if Eep will let me land.   I can find out if Eep still likes you."

Spee was touched by the Weirdling's thoughtfulness. He was so touched, he almost felt a little bad about making up her new nickname, Weirdling. Spee considered her offer.

She did strangely know things about his ship. He was not sure how, but this plan just might work. Spee finally agreed to the plan on the condition that she let Keely examine Shuey's strange belly button.

CHAPTER EIGHT

Keely pulled Shuey aside for the dreaded belly button examination. Shuey's nose was scrunched up in a cute scowl as Keely poked and prodded at her tummy.

"Goodness Shuey, look at all this stuff I'm finding in here!" Keely removed an old lollipop stick, half of a peanut, and a really tiny doll shoe. "If I didn't know any better, little lady, I'd say you've got a black hole for a belly button!"

"Hey, I was saving that!" Shuey grabbed the peanut half and tossed it in her mouth before Keely could stop her. "Besides, black holes can't be belly buttons Keely. That's impossible." Shuey pulled her shirt down before Keely could find anything else.

"I'm not finished with that," Keely tried to continue, when she heard a strange noise. "Did your belly button just cough?"

"No way.   You're crazy Keely."   And with that, Shuey took off running down the corridor before her secret was discovered.

Nearby in the control room, Spee was plotting a course to the first destination. The water planet, Planet 58293X is considered one of the most dangerous places to visit.

Why would anyone visit this planet you ask?   Squid!!!! Thousands of glowing squid-like creatures live in its seas and the source of their glow is a rare and valuable substance their body creates that can be used as a power source.

Many have risked death to gather it but few have succeeded.

Bleek was studying the squid creatures over Spee's shoulder. Spee glanced at the coordinates and then looked at

Bleek with a frown.

"Did you guys know that this planet can only be reached through a time dilation tunnel?" Spee asked Bleek and Keely.

"Looks like you'll be dropping me off at my ship before you go," Keely said with raised eyebrows. She had other clients to see and did not have time to travel with them through one of those tunnels.

"What's a time dilation tunnel?" Bleek wondered out loud.

"Time is slower inside the tunnel than it is on the outside, which means this mission is going to take longer than I expected," Spee continued to calculate as he explained.

Bleek watched as a complex equation loaded onto Spee's large screen and calculated the time it would take.

Spee's mouth emitted an actual noise in frustration when the equation was solved and projected a 7-month journey to the planet.

Keely hugged Bleek and Shuey before transporting back to her ship. She noticed how Shuey and Bleek were growing up so fast, and she predicted that the next time she saw them, they would not be children anymore.

Bleek told Keely he was going to miss her and Shuey promised Keely that she would try to keep her belly button clean.

Spee quickly installed a new defense weapon on Keely's ship just in case she ran into trouble again, and in exchange Keely donated some medical supplies for their journey.

After leaving Keely on her ship, they stopped at a nearby planet for supplies and began their journey.

Their trip through the time dilation tunnel was uneventful.

Bleek passed the time by learning as much as he could from Spee about the ship. He also learned to fire various weapons and practiced on asteroids and space junk when they would occasionally drop out of warp speed.   Spee studied the blueprints the entire time and enjoyed teaching Bleek what he knew about space travel.

We're not quite sure what Shuey did the entire time. She disappeared a lot but somehow gained the ability to yodel and liked to torture Spee with the noise as his ears were too evolved and could not handle such a sound.

When they finally reached Planet 58293X, Spee cloaked his ship and entered orbit. They loaded the shuttle with supplies and prepared to head down to the planet's surface.

The planet had a slightly purple glow that would turn a slight pink color when the light from a nearby sun would reflect off of the purple-looking water.

"Is there any land down there at all?" Bleek tilted his head and asked as he studied the planet. It appeared to be growing bigger as they approached.

"No, all water down thaaaaaaaaaar," Spee responded. The trio looked at the translator box, perplexed at the strange noise it had just made.

Shuey and Bleek giggled as Spee picked up the translator box and shook it.   Spee shrugged and set it back down.

The shuttle landed easily on the purple water, and Spee encouraged Bleek and Shuey to go out on the deck to check things out. The sun was beginning to set and as the light slowly disappeared, they could see dim lights moving down in the water.

When it was finally dark, the long tendrils of the squid creatures could be seen slowly undulating in the water.

"How are we going to catch them?" Bleek asked Spee.

"Aaaaayyye, that's a good question," Spee glared at the malfunctioning translator box.

Shuey giggled and pointed out that the translator box was making Spee sound like a pirate. Bleek found this hilarious so they began to talk like pirates too.

"Aaaaayye Captain!" Bleek shouted and pointed in front of them toward no place in particular, "Onward!"

Spee was not amused.

Spee first tried to catch the creatures with various nets but the creatures were too big and ripped through the netting. Next Spee tried to lure one into the bottom of the shuttle but the creatures appeared to be uninterested in anything Spee used as lures. Spee was becoming more frustrated by the minute and it did not help that the translator box malfunctions were becoming worse.

Spee was in the middle of a pirate-themed temper tantrum when Shuey spotted something strange on the horizon.

"Arrrrrrr!" Spee was yelling and throwing nearby objects.

Shuey waited for him to stop, walked over and tapped him on the shoulder.

"Um, Spee," Shuey said to him quietly, "What's that?"

Spee froze momentarily to turn and observe where Shuey was pointing.

"You're going to want to turn off your electronics now," a voice from the water below advised.

Spee, Shuey and Bleek all gazed down to see an old man in a rowboat below. He was fully dressed in a scuba suit, minus the mask. An oxygen tank sat next to him on the floor of his boat. The three space travelers looked at him in disbelief, all wondering where he came from.

"Hey, I'm completely serious. Turn off your damn electronics now! You have about 30 seconds before you and your ship get destroyed by planetary defense systems," he yelled at them.

Shuey ran back inside the shuttle and turned everything off. The ship's hum lowered into complete silence and became dark.

Bleek's eyes grew wide at how much brighter the creatures in the water appeared in the darkness. Suddenly a search light was on them and they could hear a soft whirring noise that grew louder as it neared them. The search light dimmed and hovering over the water before them was a massive robot with a glowing blue eye. Rows of glowing lights resembling the creatures below lined its chassis.

"Identify yourself," the robot demanded in a deep robotic voice.

"Melvin from Float Town," the old man announced from the rowboat.

Spee and his companions froze and said nothing.

"Identify yourself or exit the planet immediately," the robot voice bellowed above them.

Bleek was the first to speak up, "I'm Bleek from Istala and these to ar…"

"Silence Bleek from Istala. Your interloper companions must identify themselves."

Shuey was next to introduce herself, "I'm Shuey from Earth."

Spee gasped and the translator box translated his gasp into a "Arrrrrgh!"

"It all makes sense now, matey!" Spee exclaimed. "But wait?" he thought, "Earthlings do not grow up on space ships." Spee frowned in Shuey's direction.

The robot emitted an alarming noise. "Fourth entity identified as a pirate. Commence destruction immediately."

Spee's arms flew up and around his face in defense, "I be a land lubber matey. We're only here looking for ye treasure!"

Melvin from Float Town shook his head and planted his face in his palms. The robot's weapons powered up and prepared to fire.

"Wait!" Bleek yelled at the robot. "We're not pirates. This is Spee from, well he doesn't have a home right now but he can't talk to you without that box and it's been malfunctioning since we got here."

"Unidentified box is forbidden technology. Please move

aside Bleek from Istala," the robot commanded.

A blast from the robot's right shoulder weapon hit the translator box.   A few rounds of sparks flew off of it until finally it died.

Everyone looked from the box back up to the looming robot.

Shuey placed her hands on her hips and marched up to the side of the boat to confront the robot.   In a mocking robotic voice, she yelled at it, "Identify yourself!"

The robot only made some strange noises in response to her demand so she repeated herself, louder this time, "Identify yourself!"

This time the robot responded, "I am planet defense, guardian of the plasma squid."

While Shuey was keeping the robot busy, Bleek took some time to study the creatures below and got an idea. He slowly moved toward the end of the boat and dove down into the water.

Below the surface, Bleek swam as close as he dared to one of them. One of the creatures nearest to him slowly stretched out one of its tendrils toward him. Bleek reached out his hand to touch it but right before they made physical contact, he shape shifted, effortlessly mirroring the plasma squid he was now touching.

He was instantly and inexplicably able to communicate with the glowing green animal.

"Where did you come from?" the squid asked politely. Bleek could hear the creature in his own mind.

"Another planet," Bleek replied telepathically.

"Have you come to take my plasma?" it asked sadly.

Bleek sensed the animal's fear and realized how wrong they were to try and just take it.

"Can we make a trade?" Bleek tried to bargain with it.

The plasma squid swam and danced playfully around Bleek as it pondered his question.   Finally, it responded, "If you agree to help us with something, I'll call the robot off. There's no need to make a trade for plasma, because you already have it."

The plasma squid touched him gently with a tendril and Bleek realized he was currently a squid and had the plasma inside himself.

Bleek giggled, "Ok, deal!"

Bleek swam back up to the surface and shifted back into his regular form. He could not believe he had not already thought of this solution but was grateful for the squid's help with the robot.

The shuttle was too high so he climbed into Melvin's rowboat instead. Melvin was surprised to see him. He was even more surprised when Bleek's wiener fell off.

"Oh, hey look!" Melvin said in disbelief. "It's a worm! Can I have that for fish bait?"

CHAPTER NINE

As soon as Bleek had left the water, the robot had apologized for inconveniencing them and had excused himself to finish patrolling the area. Spee was scratching his head when Bleek yelled at them from the rowboat.

"Hey guys, down here!"

"What are you doing down there?" Shuey asked him.

"I went to talk to the squid. They want us to go back to Float Town with Melvin. They need our help," Bleek explained.

Spee began moving his arms and making strange noises but they could not understand him. He kicked a nearby fishing net in frustration.

"Maybe you should stay behind and fix that box," Bleek suggested to him, "And don't worry, I've got the plasma!"

Spee jumped up and down excitedly, picked up the box and ran into the shuttle to work on it. Shuey climbed down the side of the ship and got into the rowboat with Bleek and Melvin. Melvin was busy searching through his pack for a container to put the worm in.

Now some of you may be questioning Melvin's motives right about now, but I assure you that he is a really sweet man and truly believes he has found a worm. Poor Melvin has never seen land and has only heard about worms from others who have visited his planet.

"Where is Float Town? Is it close?" Bleek asked Melvin.

"It's right over there." Melvin pointed nearby and started rowing towards it.

"I don't see anything," Shuey said.

"We don't have any light right now. We ran out of plasma months ago." Melvin explained, "I was out here trying to investigate when I ran into you guys."

The boat nearly bumped into a dock and Melvin had to paddle a bit to get the boat right alongside it. Bleek and Shuey could barely see anything but a few shadows.

"Bleek, what are we supposed to be doing?" Shuey was trying to make out Bleek's face.

Bleek looked around him contemplating her question and then grinned.

"We should probably go talk to the plasma squid again," He suggested excitedly. He could not wait to go back down. He had always wondered what it would be like to explore the ocean without having to worry about holding his breath.

"How do we do that?" Shuey asked.

"Follow me!" Bleek dove into the water.

Shuey watched curiously as Bleek started to glow and morph. His arms stretched out longer until they were flowing tendrils.   Shuey dove in after him to watch more closely before she gave it a try. Melvin headed to the tavern to show off his new worm. He had completely forgotten about the visitors in his excitement.

Bleek and Shuey swam deeper below the surface. Shuey was almost out of air but she was close to shifting. She could feel her body begin to transform so she did not go back for air. Within seconds, she was gliding happily beside Bleek in her new squid form. They had not seen a plasma squid since the robot left but the deeper they got, the more glowing creatures they spotted. Bleek called out to them asking what they could do to help. The same green squid Bleek had communicated with earlier approached them.

"Glad you made it!" the squid said excitedly, "Follow me."

Bleek and Shuey swam even deeper. They were not used to the pressure of the deep sea and had to stop a few times to adjust. The further down they went, the brighter it got. There were plasma squid everywhere in many different colors that all glowed. The green squid led them to an area of pods.

"This is our nursery and our cemetery," the squid explained, "We supply Float Town with plasma from our dead and in return, the town supplies us with their waste, which we use to nurse our young.   Several months ago, several of the tubes were severed by a harpoon and it has disrupted our way of life."

Bleek swam over to examine the tubes. He was relieved to find that the "poop" tubes all remained intact.   Shuey was relieved to hear this and swam over too. Even though she felt she was pretty brave, she had her limits and human waste was one of them. There were about twenty tubes coming out of some pods below. They were wound together and as Bleek followed them, he found where they had all been severed.

"What does the town use the plasma for?" Bleek questioned the green squid.

"Electronics are forbidden here. The town uses the plasma to power their homes."

Bleek studied the tubing for a bit longer.

"We need to return to our ship for supplies," Bleek explained to the green creature, "I think we need an escort though. I'm feeling pretty lost and I'm not sure I'd be able to find my way back."

The green plasma squid agreed to escort them back to the ship and wait for them.

As Bleek and Shuey returned, they shifted back into their human forms and climbed up the side of the shuttle. They could hear Spee inside working. Spee was obviously frustrated and it took Bleek a few minutes to figure out what was going on.

Spee was trying to fix the translator box with a small electronic tool. He would turn the tool on for a minute, repair something and then turn the tool off while searching the area for planetary defense robots. Bleek and Shuey scared him half to death when they showed up.

Once they had calmed him down, Bleek explained that they needed to return to the ship and described the tubing as best as he could. Spee was looking forward to returning to his ship where he would have the proper tools to fix the translator box.

Spee started the shuttle as quickly as possible and they headed back to the spaceship.

Back on board Spee's roomy vessel, he excitedly took the translator box back to his favorite lab and began working on it. Bleek and Shuey headed off to another deck to find tubing. First, they checked on deck 10 where Spee kept a lot of parts and building materials.   They found plenty of tubing but it was not long enough.

"Hey Bleek, doesn't this look kind of like the tubing we use in the meat lab?"

"Maybe. Let's go check it out."

They headed to the meat lab on deck 80. The long tubes hung from the ceiling, dripping nutrients into thick chunks of meat.

Shuey liked this place. She had always felt guilty eating meat because she loved animals, but here was slab after slab of delicious meat that did not require the death of a cute furry creature.   Bleek was already searching the lab for tubing and finally found several massive rolls of it in a nearby storage room. Together they rolled the tubing out of the room and back to the shuttle.

After securing the tubing, Shuey disappeared for a bit and Bleek headed to find Spee who was finishing up repairs on the translator box. Bleek waiting patiently until Spee turned off his soldering tool and turned the box on.

"Yay!!" Spee cried and jumped around happily. When he saw Bleek, he quickly composed himself.

"We really need to work on developing your telepathy. I shouldn't have to reduce myself to using such medieval technology," he lectured.

Bleek smiled and shook his head at him, "Did you know the plasma squid use telepathy?"

Spee shook his head no.

"I guess it's time to head back, Spee."

Spee reached for the translator box.

"Without that. You can't bring that again, are you crazy?" Bleek liked being able to boss Spee around for once.

Spee crossed his arms and pouted.

CHAPTER TEN

Spee navigated the shuttle back down to the same location. By now, the sun had come up so it was easy to find Float Town. Spee immediately shut off power to the shuttle when they neared the town.

Float Town was basically a gigantic barge with houses built on it made from shipping containers. Bleek and Shuey spotted several fishermen fishing right off of the dock. Bleek and Shuey waved but no one would wave back even though they had obviously seen them land.

Bleek shrugged and started pushing the roll of tubing out to the edge of the shuttle.   He slid a pipe through the middle of the roll and wedged the ends of the pipe against the railing so that they could just unroll the tubing off the side.

"Ready?" Bleek asked Shuey.

"Ready."

Bleek grabbed the free end of the tubing and dove in. The roll of tubing unraveled as he swam down. They morphed easily into their plasma squid bodies and swam deeper below Float Town looking for the pods. Green plasma squid noticed them and swam over to assist them.

It took most of the day but Bleek and Shuey were able to run the new tubing. The plasma squid took care of attaching the ends to the bottom of Float Town and then they headed down to attach the tubes at the pods. Bleek and Shuey noticed a large group of squid bringing in a few bodies of their dead and loading them into the pods.

As soon as the tubing was attached, plasma immediately flowed up through the tubes toward the town.

The green plasma squid thanked them for their help and urged them to return to the surface to watch the fruits of their labor. Bleek and Shuey said goodbye to him and a few baby squids that had befriended them while they were working and headed back to the surface to Spee and the shuttle.

The plasma flowed slowly and they had plenty of time to enjoy their swim. On the surface, the sun was setting again and the inhabitants of Float Town were still watching Spee suspiciously.

Just as the sun slipped over the edge of the horizon, the lights of Float Town came on. The entire city lit up with glowing iridescent colors and Spee and the worm children could hear the people chattering excitedly. A few of them even cheered.

Spee was trying to ask Bleek something but he did not know how. Shuey handed him a piece of chalk that she found in her pocket. You thought I was going to say out of her belly button, didn't you? Spee proceeded to write something on the deck of the shuttle. Unfortunately, neither Bleek nor Shuey could read Spee's language.   Spee rested his face in his hands and muffled a strange scream.

"Why don't we return to the ship so we can communicate again," Bleek suggested.

Spee grabbed the sleeve of Bleek's shirt and tugged, then he pointed back to the ocean.

"Oh, you're worried about the plasma still?" Bleek asked him.

Spee nodded.

"Do you still have that giant water tank in the jungle habitat on deck 89?" Bleek asked him.

Spee nodded again.

"Let's go then. We can harvest plasma on our way to the next mission."

"I wish we could go meet the people in Float Town," Shuey told them, "but green plasma squid told me they don't talk to outsiders."

"Why did Melvin talk to us then?"

"Green plasma squid said he's crazy and that he talks to everyone, even if we can't see them."

Spee saw a planetary defense robot approaching in the distance. Its search light was on them.

"Better make it snappy, Spee!" Bleek teased.

Spee ignored the teasing and turned the shuttle back on. They lifted off towards space just as the robot was in range.

"Identify yourself," they could hear it demanding from below.

Spee pushed the shuttle as fast as it could go and soon they were out of range of the laser beams firing from the robot's shoulder weapon.

When they returned to the ship, Spee ran to find the translator box. He turned it on and placed it in Bleek's hands.

"The first thing I'm going to do…" Spee paused to sigh in relief, "..after I figure out how to do it, is develop your telepathy."

"How are you going to do that?" the worm children both asked.

"I don't know yet! But I am a far superior being and should not have to use such medieval methods of communication!"

Bleek and Shuey giggled at him.

As soon as Spee was finished venting at them, he headed to the computer to chart a course to Captain Herp Derp's secret lab.

"This is going to take a lot of planning, but we have another six months to work while we travel," Spee prepared them.

The ship entered warp speed and headed back into the time dilation tunnel. Spee excitedly skipped to deck 89. He could not wait to see Bleek and Shuey morph into plasma squid. His mind was full of ideas for ship upgrades using this new technology and he was hoping that between his two shape shifting companions, he would have an unlimited supply of plasma.

Bleek and Shuey took turns distracting the T-Rexes with meat on the crane while the other morphed into a plasma squid. Spee quickly found a way to extract the plasma with a needle. He was also excited to learn that a little bit goes a long way. On their way back to the lab, Spee handed Bleek a disk.

"What's this?" Bleek gave Spee a funny look.

"The written language of my people. Learn it," Spee ordered.   Then he headed off to his lab for some much-needed experiment time.

CHAPTER ELEVEN

Spee's experimentation time had been very productive.

For the last five months, he had managed to come up with multiple ship applications for the plasma technology, and Bleek and Shuey were able to supply him with more than enough plasma. He upgraded his weapon system with the plasma technology, which proved to be highly effective. The engines got a plasma upgrade that made them so efficient, they cut almost a month off of their journey home.

The translator box even got upgrades. Spee was able to make two, and they were small enough for Bleek and Shuey to wear as necklaces. The necklaces would glow whenever Spee was talking to them.

Bleek had learned the written language of Spee's home world and spent most of the trip running the ship. Spee made him practice maneuvers as well as charting courses until Bleek was so good at it, Spee trusted him enough to leave him by himself and spend hours working on experiments and ship upgrades.

Shuey spent a lot of time wandering off again. Bleek questioned her about it but she told him she was spending all of her time watching instructional videos she had found that came from a place called Russia.

After questioning her further, Bleek learned that she had perfected the art of ballet and sambo and had combined them into the art of ballesambo. When he looked at her in disbelief, she danced around on her toes gracefully while landing powerful blows and kicks to practice targets she had placed nearby.

Satisfied with her answer, Bleek's suspicion subsided and he found himself impressed with her new skills.

"That might come in handy sometime," he had told her.

Spee was currently sitting in his lab planning the infiltration of Captain Herp Derp's secret base. There were blueprints on multiple monitors around him and he was running a computer simulation.

"If the base is secret, how did you get those blueprints?" Bleek asked, entering the room.

"I hacked into his ship while you two were saving Keely," Spee explained.

Spee was aware of how suddenly tall Bleek appeared.

"Did you grow overnight?" Spee asked him in confusion.

"I haven't seen you in a couple of weeks," Bleek laughed at him.

Spee thought about it and nodded. He had been too busy with his projects and had neglected them on the trip back.

"Wait until you see Shuey," Bleek added.

Spee realized that he had not seen Shuey in 5 months.

"Is she tall too?" Spee asked, making a small attempt at humor.

"Uh sorta," Bleek rubbed his head nervously. "She's got boobs now."

Bleek's face turned red and Spee was completely oblivious to it. "Boobs?" Spee asked, not really paying attention.

"Anyway," Bleek changed the subject. "Shuey and I would love to help with our shape shifting abilities if you need us to."

Spee's eyes widened excitedly at this possibility he had not considered. Then he opened an animal database and began his research.

"What do you need in order to shift into a new animal?" Spee asked him.

"I just need to study them from all angles. It helps if I can see and touch them in real life, but it's possible to do it from a video and touching some of their genetic material," Bleek described his process.

Spee nodded thoughtfully and went back to researching. Bleek returned to the control room of the ship.

Later on in the week, Spee announced that his plan was finished and summoned Bleek and Shuey, but Shuey was nowhere to be found. Spee sent Bleek off in search of her. Instead of aimlessly wandering around the ship looking, Bleek decided to use the ship scanners.

First he scanned for bio signatures. The computer search yielded thousands of bio signatures, so Bleek narrowed the search to humanoids only.

"There are three humanoids on board the ship at this time," the computer announced.

Bleek was confused by this.

"Spee is not a humanoid," Bleek told the computer. "Please show me a visual."

The computer broadcasted a scaled image of the ship with two human signatures.

"Computer, I only see two."

"There are three humanoids on board the ship at this time," the computer repeated.

"You must have a computer glitch," Bleek said.

One of the signatures was his, so the other must be Shuey's. As Bleek left the control room to meet up with her, the computer continued, "I can assure you, no glitch is detected. Would you like me to run a diagnostic?"

"Yes please!" Bleek shouted over his shoulder.

Bleek rounded a corner and stopped in his tracks. He could hear Shuey talking.

"Who is she talking to?" Bleek whispered out loud to himself.

He tried to listen but she was not very loud and was muffled by a nearby air vent. Bleek decided on a sneak attack. He approached the room slowly and as quietly as possible.

"So how do I hack that?" Bleek heard Shuey ask.

"This says to cut the red and blue wires and then splice them together," another unfamiliar voice said.

Bleek froze. Who was in there with her? Was there really another human on the ship?

"Someone is coming?" Shuey asked quietly.

Bleek heard her shuffling around and decided to enter the room. He found Shuey sitting in a chair, holding up a book.

"What are you up to?" Bleek tried to ask her nonchalantly. He worried that if he got too confrontational it might backfire on him.

"Reading, obviously," Shuey answered with a hint of annoyance.

"You can read that?" Bleek asked when he saw the unfamiliar lettering on the cover.

"Well no, but maybe I'm learning," Shuey suggested and rolled her eyes.

"Who were you talking to?" Bleek asked her curiously.

"No one.   Just myself," Shuey sighed. "I like to read out loud with different voices. It makes me feel less lonely. I think I have space madness." She looked sad as she finished her sentence.

"What's space madness?" Bleek asked. He had never heard of it.

"It's a sickness the mind gets when you're in space too long. It makes you do crazy things you wouldn't normally do and things that appear to be socially unacceptable."

Bleek digested her response. He himself had been acting weird lately too. He had not been talking to himself but he had been having a strange desire to look at Shuey's boobs. He suddenly realized how pretty she was and he had a minor breakdown.

"What's happening to me!" Bleek cried.

"What's wrong?" Shuey asked, her eyes wide with

surprise.

"I think I might have space madness too!" Bleek admitted with fear in his voice.

Shuey tried to hide her guilt for lying to Bleek. She did not really know if space madness was real or not. She had only made it up to protect her secret.

"Why would you think that Bleek? I'm sure you're fine. I was just kidding about space madness. I was embarrassed that you caught me talking to myself." Shuey tried to comfort him.

"Really?" Bleek said looking at her for reassurance.

"Yeah, really. But what is happening to you?" Shuey asked.

Bleek considered telling her for a moment but then realized that would probably be a bad idea.

"I think I might need to see Keely," Bleek concluded, "We need to go see Spee anyway. He's got a plan ready for breaking into the base."

They both stood up and headed back to the control room to find Spee.

54

CHAPTER TWELVE

When Bleek and Shuey finally found Spee, the alien had a three-dimensional holographic projection of Captain Herp Derp's secret base on display.

As Spee entered his calculations into the computer, the projection changed to reflect the new data.   Certain hallways and doorways changed color as the computer highlighted the chosen routes.

The base appeared to be inside a jaggedly-shaped asteroid. The inside of the base was laid out like a large cube with a tunnel that connected to a smaller cube. The larger cube showed three levels while the smaller cube was only one level.

Spee greeted them distractedly and started his explanation of what they were looking at.

"The only entrance to the base is on the bottom of the asteroid." Spee pointed to the middle of the bottom level of the larger cube. "We'll have to travel up two more floors and enter this tunnel to reach the vault." Spee then pointed to the smaller cube.

"That sounds easy," Bleek joked around, knowing that it was about to get more complicated.

Spee ignored him and continued, "The first level should be relatively easy. It will have hired guards with minimal training. Shuey, Bleek tells me you have invented and mastered the art of ballesambo. I have no idea what that is but it sounds impressive and Bleek has assured me that it is."

Shuey beamed at the rare compliment from Spee.

"I'm going to send you in first to take care the guards. I'll be giving you this shielded suit to keep them from hitting you with any of their weapon's fire, but it won't protect you against knives or offensive blows and kicks."

"How does it work?" Shuey asked, taking the silver suit from Spee.

"The material will help you blend into your surroundings a bit but you won't be invisible. It generates a defensive shield around itself, so anything inside it will be protected," Spee explained.

Shuey was speechless and in awe.

"The second floor is going to be a tad trickier. This floor contains hundreds of booby traps."

"Let me guess," Bleek interrupted. "I get an awesome suit that repels flames and propelled objects?"

"If you want a suit, I can make you a suit, but you'll have to take it off to turn into this creature," Spee produced an image of the ugliest creature Bleek has ever seen. "You get to study this creature. It's called a povore and it eats rock and metal. We're going to just skip this level and you get to eat through the ceiling."

"Woooow," is all that Bleek managed to mutter.

"I'll give you the video files and a DNA sample that you'll need to study the creature in a moment. The third level of the base is the lab. It will be full of scientists that work for Captain Herp Derp. I'm not sure how strong they will be physically, but they might have experiments they can use against us. This will be very tricky since I cannot predict what experiments they have or if they'll even put up any resistance."

Bleek and Shuey tried to stay focused. They knew this mission was going to be dangerous, but they were both excited about preparing for their roles.

"Lastly," Spee continued, "we have the tunnel. It is protected by a deadly robot. Looking at its schematics, it has a flame thrower and several hidden laser weapons, and apparently, a removable table that folds out with a magnetic chess set on it."

"You're joking, right?" Bleek snorted and laughed.

"I wish I was," Spee replied. "I happen to despise chess."

"What is the chess game for?" Shuey asked curiously.

"That I do not know," Spee replied. "It could be a trap, or it could just be for when Captain Herp Derp gets bored of being such a loser and needs something else to suck at."

"That might be the closest thing to a joke you've ever made," Bleek pointed out, still laughing.

Spee tried to laugh but it came out as a strange throaty noise and the translators spit out their best translation, "Har har, harty ha heh."

Bleek and Shuey laughed so hard, Spee had to wait a few minutes before he could finish. Finally, Spee handed a digital copy of the povore video files and a sample container and told them to go practice.

"Uh, Spee? Is this povore poop?" Bleek asked with disgust, holding up the sample container.

"It was all I could find," Spee shrugged. "We have a few more days before we'll arrive, so please work hard on this," Spee advised. "Oh, and you might want to brush up on your shape shifting just in case."

Bleek and Shuey were excited to begin. Shuey made herself forget about keeping her secret for the next few days and put all of her focus into training.

One evening, Shuey took a break to decorate her outfit. She took the shoes and tutu she had found with the ballet video and painted them red and black. She ripped parts of the tutu which made it look tattered and worn. Then she made a red mask to go with her outfit. By the time they arrived at the base, she was wearing the tutu, mask and shoes over her silver suit.

"You look pretty bad ass," Bleek said, grinning at her when she finally joined them in the control room.

Shuey curtsied jokingly. "I'm the ballerina of destruction!" she declared in her best macho voice.

Bleek didn't bother with an outfit except some loose-fitting pants. He was pretty sure they would just tear off anyway when he shifted into the large animal he had been practicing shifting into the past few days.

The last day he had practiced, he had torn through the ceilings in one of the decks to see how hard it would be. He ate through several layers of metal and Spee might have been really angry with him had his speed and strength not been so impressive.

Bleek was more nervous about his next bowel movement than the mission that was quickly approaching.

Spee put the ship into stealth mode before the base could detect them and they slowly approached the massive asteroid. The ship was too big to dock so Spee had planned on taking the shuttle. They quickly loaded into the smaller vessel and bravely made their approach to the secret entrance at the base of the space rock.

Though the shuttle was invisible as well, they landed as quietly and carefully as possible. They exited the craft and headed towards the first door.

"This is it," Spee told them. "Please be careful and watch out for each other."

CHAPTER THIRTEEN

Bleek opened the door for Shuey and wished her luck. Bleek and Spee did not follow her in at first and stayed behind her, out of sight.

Shuey courageously entered the room to assess the situation. There were several large humanoid guards and they reminded her of Russian mafia from earth. She grinned innocently and approached them, counting their heads. There were six of them.

"Uh, can I help you?" the nearest guard asked her with a puzzled look on his face.

"I'm looking for my daddy," Shuey said, sounding as bratty and spoiled as she could. "He missed my dance recital for the last time!"

The guards all looked at each other, shrugged and laughed at her.

"How did you get here little girl?" Another guard asked. Shuey ignored him.

"You guys want to watch me dance while I wait for my dad?" She asked mischievously.

Again, they looked at each other and shrugged.

Shuey twirled and jumped gracefully.

"Awww, that's really beautiful!" the first guard praised her. Shuey could tell he was not very bright and another guard standing next to him jabbed him in his ribcage with an elbow.

"Alright little girl, it's time for you to leave. You can't be here," one of them told her.

"I'm not a little girl," Shuey snarled, staring him down with defiance. "I'm the ballerina of destruction!"

Shuey twirled and hopped over the first guard and landed

a massive blow to his groin. The struck guard fell to the ground, writhing in pain.

"What an evil creature!" he cried.

Two more guards headed for Shuey. They were not as big as the first but Shuey had to spin and flip around them to avoid them while she planned her next move. One of them was able to grab Shuey's right leg, but she flipped around and kicked his jaw, knocking him out. The other guard nearby pulled out a laser gun and fired at her. Shuey rolled into a series of back flips to avoid the shots.

Meanwhile, Bleek and Spee had entered the room, unnoticed amongst all the commotion, and began to permanently restrain the disabled guards in Shuey's path of carnage. Ok, there haven't been any deaths yet, but Shuey is imagining carnage for motivational purposes. Please indulge her and imagine it with us.

One of the blasts from the laser gun hit Shuey's silver suit and bounced off of it, hitting another nearby guard. He grabbed his arm where the laser burnt through and cried out for his mommy.

There were three more guards left and they were beginning to panic.

"Everybody panic!" one of the guards yelled as all three of them fired at Shuey simultaneously. One of the shots hit Shuey's tutu and the tattered cloth fell to the ground and quickly burned into a pile of ash. Shuey looked at the guards in disbelief.

"Which one of you destroyed my tutu?" she asked and pointed to the smallest of the three. "It was you, wasn't it?"

She gave the guard she pointed at the meanest look she could imagine on her sweet little face and growled at him. His jaw dropped and he ran past her. Spee shot the runner with a stun gun and Bleek restrained him with metal cuffs.

The last two guards ran towards Shuey and tried to grab her but Spee stunned one of them and Bleek shifted into a povore and towered over the last guard. A string of drool dripped down Blee's povore mouth and onto the guard's head.   The guard lifted his wrists up to Bleek in surrender. Spee squealed triumphantly.

"That was fun!" Shuey shouted excitedly. Her heart was pounding from all the adrenaline coursing through her veins.

A radio on one of the guards beeped loudly and a voice called for a check-in.

The three of them looked at each other in mild panic. Shuey walked over to the radio and unclipped it from the guard's belt. A radio key just happened to be on the back and Shuey looked for the all clear code. She cleared her throat and prepared to speak in the manliest voice she could muster.

"Code 4," Shuey bellowed deeply into the radio.

"Jigs?" the voice said back. "Man up, you sound like a woman."

Shuey stuck her tongue out at the radio and headed back over to join up with Bleek and Spee for the second floor.

The three of them ascended the stairs that led to the second floor. Spee inspected the ceiling at the top of the stairs for the best point of entry. As he was scanning the ceiling, a flame thrower detached from the wall in front of them and aimed right for them.

A large stream of flames poured out and Shuey quickly ran in front of it to protect Bleek and Spee. The last of her costume burned off onto the floor leaving only her silver suit showing.

Spee finished up the scans as quickly as possible and pointed to an area above them. Bleek jumped up in povore form and began to take large bites out of the metal and rock.

Shuey felt her suit beginning to heat up uncomfortably and urged him to hurry. Bleek ate through an unplanned layer of insulation and had to take a break to puke but returned to his epic meal. It was then that Bleek reached a layer of electrical pipes and he hesitated.

"Uh guys," Shuey called out uncertainly, "I have to move now!"

Bleek decided to continue through the electrical pipes. He grunted in pain when the electricity sent several shocks through him.

Spee inspected his stun weapon and made some adjustments to some of the settings. Then Spee attempted to climb up Bleek's legs until he was high enough to shoot the flame thrower. Spee suffered a short electrical shock from coming into contact with Bleek, but was able to knock out the flame thrower with a blast from his weapon.

Shuey, now free from blocking the flame, caught Spee as he slid down Bleek's thick povore legs. For the first time, ever, Spee showed affection to Shuey by giving her a hug. Shuey froze in his unexpected embrace at first, but then after the shock wore off, she hugged him back.

By now, Bleek was chewing through the bottom of the third floor. Bleek hung his large povore body upside down and grabbed his friends, swinging them up into the hole in the floor. Then he hoisted himself up through the hole to join them.

Shuey and Spee looked up to see a group of scientists gathered around them. Bleek accidentally threw up on some nearby scientists. A strange looking bug creature scientist took a partially chewed rock slab to the head, killing him instantly. The other scientists gasped in horror. For a long moment, everyone just stared at each other, contemplating the situation cautiously, until Bleek was barfing again.

"What is your purpose here?" said one of the scientists as he stepped forward. He was mostly human looking except for a long tail that reminded Shuey and Bleek of a monkey tail.

"We're breaking into the vault," Spee admitted to them. "Are you going to try and stop us?"

The scientist with the monkey tail looked at his colleagues briefly before answering, "We are being held against our will. We will help you get to the vault if you get us out of here and drop us off at the nearest planet."

"We have a deal," Spee agreed, "And sorry about your friend there." Spee pointed to the dead bug scientist.

"His death was quick and obviously an accident. We won't hold it against you," Monkey Tail reassured them. "The robot that guards the vault has a weakness. If you can get close enough to upload this program, it will override the personality inhibitor allowing you to reason with it. The robot is a prisoner here too. We will wait for you here and assist if we can."

He handed Spee the program override.

"Sorry about your friend there," Bleek apologized to the nearby scientists after he had stopped puking and changed back into himself.

The scientists were too stunned by his transformation to respond. They talked amongst themselves, developing their own theories as to what they had just seen.

64

CHAPTER FOURTEEN

Spee motioned for Shuey and Bleek to follow him and they scurried to the hallway that led to the vault.

"Bleek, can you do me a favor?" Shuey asked.

"Sure."

"Can you yell 'Hulk Smash!' the next time you morph into the povore?" she requested with a suppressed giggle.

"What does that mean?" Bleek asked curiously.

Shuey did not know how to explain to Bleek that he resembled a certain Earth comic book hero, the Incredible Hulk, when he was in povore form.

"It's an earth thing, and it would make me laugh?"

Bleek liked the idea of making Shuey smile, so he agreed even though he did not understand the joke.

They reached the entrance to the hallway in no time and peered down its dark passageway.

"How are we going to do this?" Shuey asked Spee.

"For once I have no idea," Spee admitted, "Do either of you have any ideas?"

"I have one," Bleek announced confidently, "Shuey, how's your bird shifting? Can you fly?"

"Long enough," Shuey told him after considering her options carefully. She was not entirely certain that she could but she decided to try a leap of faith, quite literally.

"Let's do this!" Bleek entered the hallway eagerly.

Bleek walked down the long and poorly lit hallway. Spee trailed behind him cautiously.

After a while, Bleek finally heard something stirring at the end of the hallway. Lights in the hallway started to come on slowly, starting off as dim, glowing orbs. When the lights became bright enough to continue, Bleek could see a robot twice the size of his povore form looming at the end.

The robot lit up and came to life. Its bell shape whirred and moved slowly while hovering in place. A number of formidable looking weapons activated on its chassis and Bleek looked back, with mild panic, to make sure Shuey was on her way.

Shuey took Bleek's moment of terror as her cue and ran down the hallway toward them. Halfway down the hall, she tried to shift but tumbled to the floor instead. She picked herself up as quickly as possible and tried to shake it off while thinking of a way to improvise. She quickly ran back the way she came before turning around and running back towards the robot again.

Just as the spaghetti-like noodle blew out her nose, she shifted back into eagle form and flapped her new wings furiously. She was able to fly over Bleek and Spee and morphed back into herself just in time to take a rolling dive behind the robot.   Spee took advantage of her diversion to fire his stun weapon at the robot. The robot sputtered in utter confusion but did not stop moving.

Shuey still had enough time to grab the program override from where she had been carrying it in her mouth and slid it stealthily into the robot's port opening.

The robot sputtered and malfunctioned. A series of beeps sounded and the robot powered down. It slowly lowered to the ground and shut off. The whirring stopped, but only for a moment before it rebooted itself. Spee readied his stun gun just in case and Bleek prepared to shift if needed.

The robot turned around and faced Shuey.

"Will you be my mommy?" it asked her.

Shuey's eyes almost bugged out of her head, "What do you need a mommy for?"

"That mean man Captain Herp Derp put me in here and made me do things, terrible things," the robot sobbed and tried to lean its head on Shuey's shoulder but realized it was too large. Then it cried even harder. Shuey patted the side of its chassis comfortingly and the robot's crying softened into a sniffling sound even though it did not have a nose.

"There there, Mr Robot. What's your name?"

The robot perked up a little, "I am TAV!"

"Tav, if you help us out, I promise to bring you with us and take care of you. Can you help us break into that vault?" Shuey bargained with him and she pointed to the door behind them.

TAV immediately hovered over and unlocked the vault without any hesitation. Bleek and Spee glanced at each other both thinking this was way too easy. TAV moved away so they could move past him and into the vault.

The lights came on as the group entered and illuminated a large room of empty shelves and open deposit boxes with nothing inside of them. Spee shook his head in disbelief, pulling out the blueprints and looking them over. Shuey pointed to the parts and materials that they were expecting to find in there and asked TAV if he knew where they were.

"Captain Herp Derp came for those a couple of days ago," TAV informed them. Strangely he was beginning to sound more human than robot as time passed.

Spee gasped with his almost nonexistent vocal chords, "Captain Herp Derp survived?!? How will we ever find him?"

"I believe he was headed for mining planet 85462M," TAV responded.

Spee gasped again.

"Isn't that…" Bleek started to ask, but Spee interrupted him.

"We must return to the ship immediately!" Spee squealed and turned to run for the ship. His arms flailed around his head as he ran back down the way they had come.

Bleek followed him a few steps, but stopped when Shuey

hesitated. TAV was operating nervously and Shuey sensed it.

"You go ahead Bleek. TAV is too big for the shuttle. Can you please have Spee beam us out from the space dock? I want to stay with him," She suggested.

Bleek nodded and continued after Spee.

"Do you think you can make it down there ok?" Shuey soothingly asked TAV.

"Yes," TAV's response was very enthusiastic, "Sit please!"

Shuey was confused at his request at first, but then he happily started to whir and part of his chassis formed into a seat. Shuey smiled and sat down. TAV hovered back down the hallway and through the lab.

He took the long way through the second level but the defense systems and traps never engaged them. The subdued guards were starting to stir as TAV and Shuey hovered by. Shuey stuck her tongue out at the guard who ruined her tutu. The guard pretended not to see her.

"That's right," Shuey yelled at him triumphantly, "you got beat up by a girl!"

TAV uttered a funny chuckling sound and continued hovering towards the space dock.

Spee was in such a hurry that he had left behind all the scientists. They were freaking out at the dock When Shuey and TAV arrived, but Bleek was in the process of reassuring them that Spee had beaming technology.

Once Spee realized that he had left everyone behind, he slapped himself across the face and initiated the beaming sequence in the computer. The ship promptly beamed everyone aboard his roomy vessel. One of the scientists fainted because he was a huge science nerd and had never seen beaming technology before.

Bleek had to explain to the scientists that there was an emergency and they would not have time to drop them off just yet. At first the scientists were unhappy but Spee agreed to let them use his lab to pass the time. The scientists all jumped at the opportunity to use his equipment and have access to some of his extensive knowledge. Shuey discovered that Monkey Tail had been the one who created TAV.

Monkey Tail spent most of their journey to the mining planet 85462M making TAV a smaller chassis. Shuey was relieved because TAV had attempted to follow her everywhere but he was so massive that he could not, and then he would cry until she came back for him.

Bleek made friends with a scientist named Pook. She was an older humanoid that reminded him of his grandma. She specialized in jet packs and was responsible for creating the hovering mechanism on TAV. Pook promised to make Bleek the coolest jet pack in the galaxy if he got her home to her family. Bleek thought he was getting the better end of the deal but he agreed and she got to work right away designing the new prototype.

TAV's new chassis was about a foot tall and came with new software that turned him into a cooking master. Monkey Tail was obviously hungry when he designed it.

Once TAV was safely transferred to his new body, he cooked a massive feast for everyone. He was able to follow Shuey to bed afterward and cuddled up to her like a puppy. Shuey put her arm around him and drifted off into a food coma.

Bleek taught Pook a card game that his grandmother had taught him. He had spent all day making the cards out of scrap cardboard he had managed to find. Pook was not very good at the game but Bleek did not care, he was just happy to play until food comas finally took them as well.

CHAPTER FIFTEEN

Spee spent most of their journey to Planet 85462M sulking in his quarters. Everyone else seemed to be enjoying themselves and he was glad to be left alone. Keely contacted the ship to check on everyone and Spee let her know where they were headed. She agreed to meet them there.

They were now several hours from the planet and Spee was becoming increasingly anxious. He headed back to the control room to monitor everything. Bleek was already in there, studying some readings on the main computer. Spee ran to see what was up.

"We're early," Bleek told him while scratching the back of his own neck.

Spee immediately transitioned the ship into stealth mode.

"He may have already detected us, if he is here already," Spee voiced his concern.

"He is here already," Bleek studied the large 3-D image of the planet and Captain Herp Derp's ship in front of them.

"I thought for sure he could not have survived our last encounter," Spee admitted to Bleek with a hint of guilt.

Bleek listened thoughtfully but said nothing in response. He imagined that Captain Herp Derp's ship was in orbit above the planet. His ship did not have stealth technology but he probably detected their ship before they entered stealth mode. Spee scanned the orbiting ship and detected Captain Herp Derp on board.

"Good, he's still on his ship," Spee confirmed gleefully.

"Should I get Shuey?" Bleek asked, "She offered to talk to Eep for you."

Spee nodded only because he could not think of a better idea at the moment.

Bleek quickly returned with Shuey. She was wearing another elaborate costume that she had put together. This time she was dressed in really short shorts with tie-dyed leg warmers that came up almost to the hem of her shorts. A purple wizard hat rested on top of her head and her hair was woven into two braids that spilled out of either side of the magical hat.

Shuey also had a tail spilling out of a hole the back of her shorts and it was randomly flicking and curling itself. At first Bleek thought it was fake but then realized that it was moving. He started to ask her how she did it but she read his mind and grinned at him mischievously.

"I'll show you later," she whispered.

An alien that looked just like Spee was already visible on the main screen and Spee had hidden himself behind a console and was out of sight. For a long moment it appeared that everyone was just staring at each other, but then Bleek realized what was happening. He flipped the switch for long range translation and immediately they heard the alien demanding to know who they were and what their intention was.

"Go put handcuffs on Spee." Shuey whispered to Bleek.

"What!" Bleek exclaimed nervously.

"I have a plan, just go with it," Shuey tried convinced him.

"I am Ana Shuezancar of Planet Earth and I am looking for…" Shuey told the alien on the screen but stopped mid-sentence when she realized she had no clue what they were looking for. All she could remember was that it was some kind of metal.

"Bleek!" Shuey called out desperately in a whisper, "What are we looking for?"

"Quadmium bars," Bleek whispered back.

Shuey turned back to face the alien, "We are seeking quadmium bars."

The alien shook his head, "We do not trade with inferior

races from earth," he replied with a hint of impatience.

"Inferior?" Shuey stuck her nose in the air.

"Spee…what race are you?" Shuey turned around to whisper in Spee's general direction.

"Zeta Reticulan," her necklace translated Spee's response.

Shuey faced the alien again.

"If I'm so inferior, how was I able to steal a Zeta Reticulan vessel and capture one of your most wanted criminals?" she shot back at him, "I want to speak to your superior."

Spee was horrified and came running out in handcuffs shaking his head.

"You did not capture.." he tried to protect his ego, but Bleek bopped him on the head before he could finish.

"No, she did not capture you. I did, but I work for her," Bleek finished Spee's explanation for him.

The alien had his face pressed all the way up to the camera and appeared to be freaking out over Spee's appearance.

Suddenly, Spee was frozen in place and was staring up at a different alien that had appeared on the screen. Shuey and Bleek could only tell the new alien was different because it was taller.

"I am Commander Eep, I hear…" Eep trailed off when she saw Spee.

"How do you guys tell the males and females apart?" Bleek and Shuey asked Spee at the same time. Spee was too distracted to answer.

"I hear you want to make a trade?" Eep finished her sentence. The translator voice imitated her anxiousness.

"We need quadmium bars," Shuey repeated, "We are willing to trade Spee."

"Is that the name you go by these days?" Eep directed her question at Spee who still said nothing.

"I will come to you," Eep informed them.

The alien behind her started to protest but she told him

something and he backed down.

The computer notified them that someone was beaming aboard. Bleek acknowledged the alert and lowered the shields long enough to allow her to board. Spee was taking very deep breaths.

Eep was now standing in front of them, holding a satchel which she handed to Shuey.

"Your quadmium," She said, identifying the contents of the bag.

"Uh, I'm not sure what to do next, Spee," Shuey admitted meekly.

"I'm not going to take him," Eep explained, sensing the earth girl's fear. "I just need to talk to him."

CHAPTER SIXTEEN

Spee asked Bleek and Shuey to leave so that he could talk to Eep in private. He disabled their translator necklaces and shuffled them out of the room quickly.

Bleek pulled Shuey down the hall with him into another room and turned on a computer. He tinkered with the settings until he was able to access a translator program and intercept the telepathic transmissions from the control room.

Keely had recently docked with Spee's ship and had been searching for them. She spotted them dart into the room and walked in on them eavesdropping. At first, she pretended to disapprove but then she closed the door and sat down with them.

Meanwhile, in the control room, Spee and Eep discussed their uncomfortable past.

"I don't understand. Was it something I did?" was the first question Spee needed to ask her. "It was the tattoo, wasn't it?"

"I lied to you, Jek, I mean Spee," Eep explained regretfully. "I was sent to keep tabs on you for the high counsel. My name isn't even Eep. It was a cover name given to me and I kept it."

Spee was stunned and struggled to process her explanation.

"I didn't mean to fall in love with you Spee. I didn't realize I had until I saw the tattoo and then I was ashamed because our love was based on a lie," Eep continued. "I spent the journey home deciding what to do. When we arrived, I immediately asked for a transfer. You and that ego of yours are not always easy to love but I did anyway, and that's why I knew I had to let you go. I couldn't spy for them any longer. And that's why I got stuck with this job. The counsel hated me for it and used my transfer to punish me."

Spee's poor heart ached but he believed her in spite of the hurt he felt. Even though she had lied to him at first, he wanted to believe her.

"I wanted to come find you but I just couldn't," Eep told him with tears in her large black eyes.

Spee stepped closer to Eep, who was much taller than him and embraced her tightly. Eep stiffened at first, because she believed that she did not deserve his forgiveness, but Spee told her all was forgiven anyway. He gently patted her shoulder.

"You've changed a lot," Eep pointed out. "Does it have anything to do with those humans you travel with?"

"Oh Eep, I have so much to tell you. I wish I could just sit with you and catch up but I'm afraid that has to wait."

"Does this have something to do with Captain Herp Derp?" Eep asked curiously.

Spee nodded, "During our last encounter with him, we stole some blueprints off of him. I thought I had destroyed his ship but he managed to warp away and survived. We've been traveling around, collecting materials and parts needed to build the device in the blueprints. The plan was to build the alternate reality device and travel to a reality in which I had not lost favor with our home world, but Captain Herp Derp has taken some of the parts.   I believe he headed here to obtain quadmium as well."

"That explains his presence," Eep muttered thoughtfully. "He has ignored all attempts we have made to communicate with him. We've been expecting trouble from him at some point."

Spee considered Eep's new information.

"That brings me to our next issue," Eep changed the subject. "I think we might be able to use that as a way for me to return to the mining base without you."

"You're not coming with us?" Spee questioned desperately.

"I wish I could. I need to remain here until your name is cleared with the high counsel," Eep explained.

"But that isn't the plan. We're going to an alternate reality."

"You can't just run away to another reality every time things don't work out the way you think they should," Eep told Spee. She regretted saying it immediately. She had ran and now she was telling Spee not to. "You are here, in this reality, with so many possibilities. You can't give up on us yet. Build your device, but don't use it for that."

Spee considered her advice and knew she was right, even though part of him wanted to point out her hypocrisy. There was no point and no time to indulge in that kind of egotistical behavior right now.

"I have no idea how to win back the favor of the high counsel," Spee finally admitted, shaking his head and looking at the floor.

"I have been hearing rumors lately," Eep shared. Her voice was softer and Spee could sense her fear. "There is talk of a major problem on the home planet. No one seems to know details. It is all very hush hush, but they have been sending for some of our best scientists. Perhaps you could help? You're the smartest scientist they have. They won't admit it, but they need you."

"I'll look into it as soon as we get out of here," Spee assured her even though he was not yet sure that he would, "For now we need to figure out how to get out of here."

"About that," Eep began, "What if we commandeer his ship, steal the parts you need and then start a fight with the base? I'll beam back to the planet after the fight begins and take Captain Herp Derp with me. That way I won't return empty handed and you can take off without resistance from my officers."

"Oh how I've missed you," Spee squealed. "You always knew how to satisfy my taste for mischief and mayhem."

Spee hugged Eep one more time and suggested that they go find everyone to begin planning.

Bleek, Shuey and Keely were chattering excitedly in the spare room when Spee and Eep discovered that they had been eavesdropping. Normally Spee would be flabbergasted but he was too happy to have reconciled with Eep, and his hope in returning home had been renewed.

"Wait until you see my costume for this!" Shuey exclaimed. She threw a fist pump up in the air for good measure. Then she skipped down the hall yodeling and Keely caught Bleek watching her. He had a certain look in his eye and it suddenly occurred to her that Bleek and Shuey were no longer children.

CHAPTER SEVENTEEN

Spee came up with a brilliant plan to lure Captain Herp Derp away from his ship, using the quadmium bars. He figured that Captain Herp Derp was there for them anyway, and stealing them from Spee would be easier than trying to break into the mining base.

Spee set the plan in motion by sending out a fake transmission to Keely's ship requesting that she take the quadmium to a contact in a nearby galaxy. Then Spee sent out a second transmission that his beaming device was offline and they would be manually transferring the quadmium to her ship via shuttle. Eep and Spee boarded the shuttle without the quadmium and flew in the direction of Keely's orbiting ship.

Keely stayed behind on Spee's roomy vessel with Bleek and Shuey and waited for the signal. Sure enough, a smaller spacecraft left Captain Herp Derp's ship and set a course to intercept the quadmium.

Keely beamed Bleek and Shuey aboard Captain Herp Derp's ship as soon as he had left.

"Wow, he's made some serious upgrades. When did he have time to do all this?" Shuey asked in amazement after they materialized aboard the enemy's spaceship.

"Are you ok looking for these parts?" Bleek asked Shuey, pointing to the blueprints they had brought. "I'm going to get his weapon systems going."

"Yeah, can I take the paper with me?"

Shuey took the blueprints from Bleek and began her search for Captain Herp Derp's on-board lab.

Meanwhile, Eep and Spee awaited the Captain's arrival.

"Are you sure it was a good idea to send those kids to his ship alone?" Eep asked Spee with genuine concern.

"Oh, they can hold their own," Spee assured her. "They are my greatest success to date!"

Eep studied Spee for a moment. "You're not going to win back favor of the high counsel experimenting on children," she argued peacefully.

"You are right, Eep, but what you do not know is that I saved them from certain death. Then I made a deal with them, giving them permission to live on my ship if they allowed me to conduct my experiments," Spee explained. He could see no problem with the arrangement whatsoever.

"What did you do to them anyway?"

"You wouldn't believe me, but I will show you one day," Spee promised her.

Captain Herp Derp boarded the shuttle just as Spee finished his sentence.

"Shhhhh!!" Captain Herp Derp said involuntarily as he made his presence known to them.

Spee rolled his eyes.

"Where ith the quadmium?" the Captain demanded.

"I've got some quadmium for you right here," Eep said as she slapped some quadmium alloy wrist restraints on him.

"Noooooooo," he cried and glared at Spee, "You alwayth ruin everything!"

Shuey was searching the lab when TAV contacted her from the ship.

"Mom, are you coming back soon?" TAV asked through the translator necklace.

"Not yet puppy, what's up?"

"She left the room. I couldn't stop her," TAV reported.

"What?!" Shuey said in disbelief, "Where did she go?"

"She said something about the scientists and Monkey Tail and a cure."

"You have to get her back TAV. No one can see her. Please TAV!" Shuey was panicking. She did not have time for this right now.

"Ok mom, I'll go find her."

"Hurry TAV, this is really important!" Shuey pleaded just as she found the parts she had been searching for.

"Yes!" She grabbed the materials and turned around to find Bleek standing in the room with his arms crossed and a look of disappointment on his face.

"What was that all about?" he asked her.

"Oh nothing, just one of the scientists," Shuey lied.

"Shuey," Bleek began to say, trying not to feel hurt by her obvious lie, "I thought we were friends. You can trust me, I promise."

Shuey lowered her face to the floor and handed the parts to Bleek, "I promise I'll explain everything once we complete this mission."

"You swear?"

"I swear Bleek."

Bleek did not look satisfied with her answer but they needed to head back to the control room and radio Keely.

"We're ready. Has Spee contacted you?" Bleek radioed when they had returned to the control room on Captain Herp Derp's spaceship.

"Yes, just now. They have apprehended him and are returning. I'll signal you when we're ready," Keely advised.

After returning to his ship, Spee and Eep ushered Captain Herp Derp out of the shuttle to be greeted by a gauntlet of pissed off scientists.

"Feed him to the T Rex!" one of them shouted.

"Treacherouth interloperth!" Captain Herp Derp shouted at them, "Shhhhhh!"

A giant piece of poop flew through the air and hit him in the face. Spee jumped out of the way just in time and observed in horror as the turd rolled off onto the floor.

We're pretty sure it was Monkey Tail who threw it, for obvious reasons, but he denies it to this day.

"We're ready, Keely," Spee notified her when they had finally returned to the control room.

"Bleek. Shuey. We're ready when you are." Keely sent her transmission and tapped her fingers anxiously. She did not like the thought of them in so much danger.

"Copy that, weapon sequence has been initiated. We are ready for pick up now," Bleek replied as he finished pushing a few buttons.

Keely immediately beamed them aboard. A few seconds later, a large laser beam shot up from the planet and obliterated Captain Herp Derp's ship.

"I curth you! Curth you!! Shhhhh!" the Captain shouted at Spee. He wailed loudly with grief at the loss of his spaceship and its contents.

Spee did not hear him though because Eep was waving goodbye to him sadly. He was not ready to part with her yet but he knew that he must for now. Everyone waved goodbye to Eep as she beamed back down to the mining base with Captain Herp Derp.

"Oh crap! I forgot the devices!" Bleek yelled out in panic. He glanced around him looking for them desperately, hoping he had just misplaced them.

"What?!?!" just about everyone in the room yelled back at him.

"Kidding!" Bleek said holding them up and grinning.

Spee sighed with relief. As soon as he had recovered from Bleek's mean prank, he excitedly grabbed the parts and the quadmium bars and headed for his lab to build the device.

"Set a course for Zeta Reticuli!" Spee commanded as he left the room.

Bleek made some calculations on the computer and Shuey tried to sneak off.

"Ahem," Bleek cleared his throat to let Shuey know that he noticed her leaving.

Shuey grimaced and stopped in her tracks. "It would be better if I showed you," Shuey finally said with defeat.

"After you." Bleek locked in their destination motioned for Shuey to lead the way. He followed her patiently back to her room.   He was anxious to learn about this secret she had been keeping for a long time.

CHAPTER EIGHTEEN

In all the excitement, Shuey had briefly forgotten about TAV contacting her, but now she remembered. She took off running down the hallway to her room. For a moment Bleek wondered if she was running away from him but he quickened his pace to keep up with her.

"TAV!" Shuey yelled out for him as soon as she entered her room. A look of relief enveloped her face when she found him waiting for her.   "Did you find her?"

"Yes, Mom. I convinced her to come back with me."

"Will you please just tell me what's going on?" Bleek requested impatiently.

"Go ahead and show him, TAV."

TAV hovered down off of Shuey's bed and stopped directly in front of Bleek. A small compartment in TAV's chassis opened and a very tiny person emerged.

"Holy…" Bleek was almost too shocked to speak. "Is that Steph, from my school?" Bleek recognized the tiny girl as one of his classmates that Spee had rescued.

"I thought you were dead!" Bleek told her in disbelief. "What happened to you?"

"That horrible Spee performed one of his experiments on me. He thought I died too, but I didn't. I shrank so much he just couldn't see me. Then I hid and thought it was best to just keep hiding. Shuey found me one day while you two were exploring the ship," Steph explained. She was so happy to talk to someone else. She adored Shuey and TAV but she was excited to have someone new to interact with.

"So that's why the computer was malfunctioning. It kept telling me there were 3 humans aboard the ship." Bleek was putting the pieces together finally.

"And that's why you kept hearing me talking to someone," Shuey admitted to Bleek, then looked at Steph with concern. "Why did you leave the room?"

"TAV told me there were scientists on the ship. I was hoping one of them could reverse my condition." Steph tried to defend her actions. "I want to be a normal girl again.   I want to be with you."

Bleek was incredibly confused and looked to Shuey for further explanation.

"She's my girlfriend," Shuey confessed. She smiled meekly.

A piece of Bleek died inside of him when he heard this. He hid his disappointment as best as he could.

"We should tell Spee," He tried to convince them. "He did this, and he's the only one who can undo it."

"No!" Shuey objected sharply. "What if something happens and I lose her?"

"I don't think that's your call," Bleek said, glancing at Steph.   He had to squint to read the look on her face and she looked incredibly torn.

After a few minutes of thinking it over, she gave them her verdict. "I'd rather die than be this small for the rest of my life."

Shuey sighed in defeat. "Alright, let's tell him."

She carefully reached down and picked Steph up and put her in the pocket of her pants. Then she proceeded to walk as slowly as possible in the direction of Spee's lab.

Keely followed Spee to his lab. She had something important to tell him, and she was deciding how to tell him along the way. When she found him, she watched him skipping joyfully about his lab as he assembled the device.

"Um, Spee?" She tried to get his attention.

"Hmmm?" Spee responded absentmindedly.

"The children, well, the kids, er…" She searched for the

words she was looking for and realized he was not listening.

"Spee!" She yelled loudly, slapping a nearby table top.

Spee was shaken from his creativity. "What?" He appeared to be mildly annoyed with her for interrupting his special lab time.

"Bleek and Shuey. They aren't kids anymore."

Spee looked up at her and tilted his head. He was not sure why she was telling him this.

"Have you talked to them about it at all?" Keely asked.

"Why would I talk to them about it?" Spee replied with a question, completely missing the point.

Keely tried to find a metaphor he would understand, "Ok, what about your dinosaurs. They aren't children, so you had me um…fix them so that you wouldn't have a herd of baby dinos taking over your ship."

Spee jumped up and down excitedly when he realized his most successful experiment was ready for the next stage. "Oh! It's time to breed them!" he announced gleefully, clapping his hands.

"So, you DO want more worm children?" Keely was confused. She thought Spee would have been concerned and not excited.

"Yes! The experiment I performed on them is very costly. If I am to profit from this experiment on my home planet I will require many worm children. That's why I chose a female for the second one."

Keely tried to grasp what Spee was explaining to her.

"Why would your home world want worm children?" She was positively perplexed.

"We often steal human reproductive samples to create more of us. We take the samples and modify them. If we have worm children, we will have an unlimited supply of superhuman reproductive samples. Imagine all of the scientific applications! A whole army of Zeta Reticulans who are able to shape shift from birth," Spee said passionately.

Keely finally realized how clueless Spee was. She thought he genuinely cared for Bleek and Shuey but now she was almost certain he only cared about his status on his home planet. She considered giving him a piece of her mind, but Spee had already halted the creation of the device and was leaving to search for his shape shifting experiments.

Bleek and Shuey saw Spee approaching them. TAV was close behind his mommy like a good puppy. Shuey removed Steph from her pocket and held her gently in her left palm.

"I have wonderful news!" Spee exclaimed, "It's time for you two to procreate. I need more worm children."

Bleek and Shuey's eyes both widened with panic and Shuey closed her hand around Steph protectively.

"What the hell are you talking about?" she demanded.

Bleek's face turned a dark shade of red. He admitted to himself that he would be all for it, but not like this. Not with Shuey and Steph being together, and both lesbians. Bleek turned an even darker shade of red. He then quickly shape shifted into a small turtle to hide the boner he had thinking about lesbians. He prayed that no one had seen it.

"Why is this happening to me?" Shuey's translator necklace picked up on Bleek's turtle dialog.

"I don't understand what the problem is," Spee looked from the turtle on the floor back to Shuey. "You should instinctively know to make small miniature versions of yourself. It's in your DNA."

"I am not procreating with a boy!" Shuey yelled angrily at Spee. "Gross!"

"Oh not this again," Spee retorted in frustration. "Keely cured your cooties."

Bleek shifted back again, praying that his wiener would fall off and takes its precious time growing back. Without warning, Spee swiftly grabbed both of their hands. He did not notice that as he grabbed Shuey's left hand, he sent the tiny Steph flying through the air.

"Nooooo!" Shuey cried. She tried to pull away from Spee to run and catch her but he was a lot stronger than she had expected.

TAV hovered around trying to judge Steph's trajectory. His programming kicked in and he hovered over and caught her before she splattered.

"Good boy TAV!" Shuey cried as Spee attempted to drag them off to who-knows-where.

CHAPTER NINETEEN

Bleek and Shuey worked together to knock Spee over and make a run for it. They made it to the nearest hall intersection just in time for Spee to whip out his stun gun and shoot both of them simultaneously.   They were too heavy for him to carry so he called Keely for help.

"Spee!" Keely shouted in dismay when she arrived, "What are you doing?"

"They refuse to procreate!" Spee yelled back at her in frustration.

"You can't just order them to do that!"

"Why not?"

"They aren't animals, they're humans."

"Just help me get them into a holding cell," Spee ordered her.

"Fine. I'll help you get them there. I'll give you 24 hours to try and make them procreate and then I'm letting them out," Keely bargained with him.

"Fine," Spee agreed, only to convince her to help. He had no intention of letting her release them after 24 hours unless they had successfully mated.

Keely used one of her gurneys to help move the temporarily paralyzed Bleek and Shuey. TAV followed behind his mom, silently observing and wishing he could do something to help her.

Bleek and Shuey could move everything above their necks by now, but they refused to speak. Shuey was full of worry and rage. She wanted to check on Steph but she was afraid of Spee finding out about her now. What would he do to Steph if he found out she liked a girl and not Bleek. Would he "accidentally" kill her?

"TAV?" Shuey asked quietly, "Is everything ok?" She tried to word it inconspicuously.

"Everyone is present and accounted for," TAV responded enigmatically.

"I thought we were friends, Spee," Bleek finally said.

Spee felt a small and sudden pang of guilt but chose to ignore it. He did save Bleek's life and for that Bleek owed him his life. He did not understand why they were being so ungrateful for the mercy he had shown by saving them in the first place.

Keely felt like she was an accomplice to a kidnapping and it was breaking her heart. As soon as Bleek and Shuey were as comfortable as possible in their holding cell, Keely stormed off down the hallway. She wanted to cool off for a moment and figure out how to best help them.

"You two are not coming out of there until she is pregnant!" Spee informed them, pointing at Shuey. Then he turned around and returned to continue working on the device.

"I'm so sorry about all this," Bleek confided in Shuey after Spee had left.

"Why are you sorry? It's not your fault," Shuey comforted him. "What if we just tell him we did it?"

"He has a scanner for that. I saw him use it on the female T Rex to confirm she was pregnant," Bleek said, squashing Shuey's hope.

TAV hung out in front of the cell like a loyal puppy. Steph exited her secret compartment and climbed on top of TAV's head.

"Just tell him Shue," Steph pleaded with her.

"I don't trust him!" Shuey stated. "I'm afraid he'll kill you and make it look like an accident."

Bleek would have normally stood up for Spee but now he wasn't so sure. He had not seen Spee like this since he first began performing his experiments on the class.

Over the next several days, Shuey and Bleek hung out in their holding cell. TAV and Steph settled in a spot on the floor in front of their holding cell and occasionally brought them food.

Steph, who had grown up on Bleek's home planet, had spent lots of time with her father on his spaceship. He was a trader and she had learned how to fix and maintain the ship at an early age. She had been the one teaching Shuey how to hack and operate Spee's systems.

She used her knowledge to try and open the holding cell but it was proving difficult. She had to hide anytime someone approached. She cursed at the computer console when she realized she could not hack it.

After the first twenty four hours, Keely hunted Spee down and demanded that he release them. Spee refused.

"I don't understand what has happened to you," Keely said to him. She was beginning to feel desperate and out of control.

Spee ignored her and told himself that he did not have to answer to anyone. Once he impressed the high counsel, they would welcome him back and he would be too busy to talk to these ship companions of his that were behaving so selfishly. He did not understand why it seemed like no one wanted him to succeed.

Keely spent the second day trying to free them. She tried figuring out the controls by herself but they were a lot different than the ones on her ship. She attempted asking Bleek for help but they could not hear each other through the barrier. Then she noticed TAV beaming food into the cell. Bleek and Shuey were not feeling hungry but they ate out of boredom. TAV had given them his old chess set from his previous chassis, but they grew tired of the game quickly.

"Hey TAV, do you think you could beam this in there?"

Keely asked the robot while holding out a communication device.

TAV excitedly beamed the gift into the cell and sighed happily after doing so. He felt like he was helping them. Bleek and Shuey playfully fought over who would get to use it first. A quick rock, paper, scissor duel ended with Bleek as the victor.

"Hey Keely!" Bleek said into the device.

Keely heard his greeting through a second device that she kept.

"Walkie Talkies, eh?" Bleek pointed at the device with a goofy grin.

"Walking Whaties?" Keely repeated what she thought she heard. "Is that what humans call these things?"

Bleek and Shuey giggled.   They were relieved to finally be able to talk to another friend again.

"I'm trying to get you guys out. I'm so sorry about all this. I'm sorry about helping him. I thought he would let it go after a day or so. I have no idea what's gotten into him," Keely apologized, "What buttons do I press to get you out of here?"

Bleek shook his head at her solemnly. "He locked it with a retinal scan. We're not getting out of here without Spee."

Keely sighed in frustration. Shuey asked Bleek for the communication device.

"Keely?" Shuey asked quietly with a quiver in her voice.

Keely's heart broke when she heard it. "Talk to me Shuey."

"Why do I have to procreate with Bleek?"

"You don't have to do anything you don't want to, dear."

"Why does Spee think we need to?"

"Because he's a self-absorbed idiot," Keely answered angrily.

"I need to tell you something. Please don't be mad."

"I'm not going to be mad at you Shuey."

"I don't like boys."

Keely's eyes widened as it sunk in slowly. Shuey suddenly made perfect sense to her.

"You're mad aren't you?"

"No, Shuey. I think I understand you better than I ever have."

"One more thing. Please don't be mad."

Keely was still processing Shuey's first bombshell and was not sure she was ready for another surprise. However, she sensed that Shuey really needed her to listen.

"I have a tiny girlfriend that I used to hide in my belly button but now TAV takes care of her."

Keely did not believe her at first, but then TAV opened the secret compartment in his chassis and Steph peeked her head out and waved at everyone. Keely finally understood why she had found half of a peanut in Shuey's belly button. Tiny people need to eat too.

CHAPTER TWENTY

Spee was working on the device when Keely came looking for him again. He sensed her presence but continued working. He wondered if she would go away if he ignored her.

"Spee, this has to stop," Keely said gently.

Spee had already been contemplating giving up on the human breeding experiment. Guilt was eating away at him but pride was keeping him from giving it up just yet. Keely sensed this and thought carefully about what to say next. She did not want to hurt his pride any further and risk having this go on any longer than it already had.

After organizing her thoughts in her head, she began with an angle that might soften him up a little.

"You love Eep, right?" she asked.

"Most definitely."

"You would procreate with her if you could, right?"

"We don't have reproductive organs."

"But if you did, you would?"

Spee was thoughtful for a moment. "Yes."

"Shuey has an Eep, but it's not Bleek," Keely broke the news to him.

Spee looked slightly confused so Keely tried to explain it better. "She loves someone. She would rather procreate with the person she loves than her friend Bleek."

"Who does she love?"

"Her name is Steph."

"I fail to see where they could procreate with each other. They do not have the corresponding body parts."

"Neither do you and Eep," Keely patiently argued.

Spee finally understood. He stopped fiddling with the

device and actually looked at Keely.

"I am such an idiot," he admitted sadly. "Who is this Steph? Have I met her?"

"You have, but I'm not sure you'd remember her."

"When?"

"Spee, you should go let them out of the holding cell. Perhaps it would be a good idea for you to discuss this with Bleek and Shuey," Keely wisely advised him.

"You're right, Keely. Thanks for talking some sense into me."

Keely, sensing how terrible Spee felt, rested a hand his shoulder. "You can make this right. I know you can."

Spee set his tools down and headed towards Bleek and Shuey's holding cell while contemplating what he was going to say to them. When he reached their cell, TAV muttered a string of expletives at him in a robotic language that no one was familiar with.

Spee entered a password to unlock the cell and wondered if the translator necklaces had translated what TAV had just said.

"I..I'm sorry," Spee stuttered when the door opened.

Neither Bleek nor Shuey could look him in the eye.

"I was wrong to force you two into doing something you didn't want to," Spee continued. "I was only thinking of myself and my status with the high counsel. I forgot who my real friends were."

A tear fell down Shuey's cheek and she sniffled. Steph heard Shuey crying from inside her secret compartment. She could even hear the large tear as it hit the floor and splashed somewhere outside of her safe hiding spot.

"TAV, let me out!" a small voice cried out from inside of him. TAV tried to make a series of beeps and noises to cover it up, but Steph would not give up.

"TAV! LET ME OUT!" the voice repeated really loudly. Steph banged loudly on the inside of TAV's chassis.

"Let her out TAV. It's ok," Bleek reassured the puppy-like robot.

TAV looked to Shuey for guidance but she was slumped over on the floor. Finally, he released Steph.

Spee watched in fascination as TAV hovered over to Shuey and allowed Steph to climb onto Shuey's lap. The tiny human was so small that she could barely wrap her arms all the way around Shuey's thumb in a hug. Shuey leaned down and gently kissed the top of Steph's head. Then Shuey picked up her girlfriend, tucked her away gently into her palms and stood up.

"Because of you Spee, I can't even hug my girlfriend without squashing her," Shuey cried and left the room.

TAV hovered after her, comforting her with cute nurturing robot noises.

"Where did the tiny human come from?" Spee asked Bleek.

Bleek was too hurt to reply. He tried to tell Spee how he felt a couple of times but then decided he was feeling too betrayed to have this discussion right now. Instead, he shook his head sadly at Spee and left to find Pook. He needed to talk to her and he knew she would listen.

Spee's guilt made him feel about as small as Steph. Instead of wallowing, he decided to research the tiny human. After several minutes of scanning and consulting his experiment archives, he discovered that Steph was one of Bleek's classmates. He thought she had ceased to exist after using a phase-displacement tool on her. Had he absentmindedly used a shrink ray gun on her instead?

He then made his way to the storage container that was keeping the phase-displacement tool. He spent the next few hours trying to reproduce the experiment on several lab animals, but the tool was moving them in and out of phase as intended. Spee was stumped.

Spee considered his next move carefully. He wanted to fix

his mistake and make amends. He realized that he would rather have his human friends back then suck up to the high counsel and be welcomed back home. He also realized that he had had more of a home on his ship with Bleek and Shuey than he ever did back home.

Spee experienced a moment of clarity in which he felt that he knew exactly what he needed to do. First, he would reroute the ship to take all the scientists on board home, and he would enlist their help returning Steph to her previous size on the way. Spee felt a glimmer of hope inside himself.

He would make this right if it was the last thing he ever did.

CHAPTER TWENTY-ONE

Pook was in one of the labs working by herself when Bleek found her.   He knocked on the door softly to avoid startling her. She smiled at him warmly and motioned for him to come look at what she was working on.

"It's almost finished!" she announced excitedly and pointed at the jet pack in front of her.

"Wow! Can I try it out when it's finished?" Bleek asked.

"I made it just for you, Bleek."

He ran his fingertips down the sleek and shiny metal. It was painted white and silver and had a blood-red worm painted on the back in the center. Bleek chuckled because the worm had a giant mouth full of sharp and scary looking teeth.

"I made up a logo for you." Pook giggled at her handy work.

"I love it, Pook. Thanks!"

"I should have it ready before Spee drops me off at home."

Bleek took one more look at the jet pack and moved out of the way to let Pook continue working on it. He walked over to a nearby stool and took a seat. There was paper and pencils on the table in front of him and he started to draw. He found it soothing after spending the last few days locked in a cell. He wondered how Shuey and Steph were doing.

"I heard you had a rough few days," Pook told him as she continued to work on the wiring in the jet pack. "Do you want to talk about it?"

"It was pretty humiliating," Bleek admitted.

"You have a crush on Shuey, don't you?"

Bleek's face turned bright red. He could feel the heat collecting in his cheeks and on the back of his neck.

"It's alright. We don't have to talk about it, but if you want to, I promise whatever you say won't leave this room," Pook reassured him.

Bleek took a couple of deep breaths to prepare himself to talk about it. He knew he could count on her to listen without judgment.

"Yeah, I do like her, a lot," He finally confessed. "I've never felt anything like it before. But it doesn't matter, because she likes someone else."

Pook nodded her head in understanding, "You probably won't believe me, but it's not the last time it will ever happen. There will be others."

"I thought Spee was my friend," Bleek said, changing the subject to what was hurting him the most.

Pook paused to look up at him for a moment.

"Have you ever let anyone down before?" she asked him.

Bleek was thoughtful for a moment. He thought back to the day everything had changed on his planet. "I hurt my mom's feelings before I went to school one day." Bleek tried not to cry as he remembered what happened. "She told me I couldn't go to a friend's house that weekend because she was worried about some stuff and wanted me to spend time at home with her and my dad. I was really mad, so I told her she was a horrible mom and then I left for school. I never got to see her again and I never got to say I was sorry. There was a nuclear war. We saw these clouds shaped like mushrooms and felt really huge tremors. We were scared and our teachers were trying to figure out what to do. Part of the building collapsed and blocked our way down any hallways. That's when Spee beamed my classroom up to his ship."

Pook continued to listen intently while fiddling with her project. Bleek drew the mushroom clouds that he had seen back then while he was telling her his story. He picked up the paper and showed it to Pook. She stopped working and walked over to him to get a better look and then gave him a comforting hug.

"Your mom knew you didn't mean it. You were just a kid who wanted to have fun with his friends. You said some hurtful things and then you learned something important, right?"

"I learned that you can lose anyone at any time for any reason, and that it's important not to lose sight of what's really important. I learned that whatever I say to someone could be the last thing that they ever hear," Bleek told her.

"Perhaps Spee is learning a similar lesson right now," Pook suggested wisely.

Bleek nodded, "You're right. He probably is, but I don't know if I'm ready to forgive him yet."

"You take all the time you need," Pook said and rubbed his arm gently before returning to her work.

Bleek went back to drawing.

"Thanks Pook."

"Anytime!"

Steph helped Shuey thread a needle.

Shuey smiled down at her. "And that's why I keep you around," she said playfully. "Who needs a needle threader when I've got you?"

Steph was happy that Shuey was smiling again.

"What are you making, mom?" TAV asked.

"My new ballerina-of-death costume," Shuey said in silly voice.

"It's going to be waaaay better than the first one," Steph added.

Steph had drawn the new design to cheer her girlfriend up. Shuey had had to use a magnifying glass to look at it, but her spirits were instantly lifted as soon as she saw it. It reminded Shuey of a book she read when she was a kid.

"We had a book on my planet called 'The Indian in the Cupboard.' It's about a boy who puts a plastic toy in a cupboard and locks it. When he opens the cupboard, the Indian is alive," Shuey told Steph. "I feel like I'm in that book right now. I have my own toy human that hangs out with me."

"What's an Indian?"

"Indians are awesome!" Shuey said excitedly. "Although now we call them Native Americans. A man named Columbus thought he had sailed around the world to a place called India, and that's why he named them Indians, but it turned out that he had sailed to a place he had no idea existed. They wore leather shoes called moccasins and wore feathers in their hair. They rode horses and hunted buffalo and other animals for food. They were one with nature! When I was a kid I wanted to be one. My grandmother studied our family tree and discovered that I was 1/356th Cherokee Indian. I was so excited to have even that small amount."

Steph loved hearing things about Shuey's planet even though she had to ask a lot of questions because she did not understand everything.

"This is why I love having a girlfriend from another planet!" Steph said happily.

Shuey continued to think about the book as she sewed her new costume. Then she had an idea. She decided that she would surprise Steph by building a tiny Native American village for her.

CHAPTER TWENTY-TWO

Monkey Tail analyzed Spee's data from the experiments on Bleek's classroom.

"Interesting," he muttered as he scrolled through the data on the screen in front of him.

Spee tinkered with the phase-displacement device and patiently waited for Monkey Tail to read everything.

"What's this tool?" Monkey Tail asked, pointing at a device on the screen.

Spee gasped because it looked very similar to the phase-displacer. "That's a personal protection device!" he exclaimed. "I need to go talk to Steph."

Spee took off running out of the lab before Monkey Tail could ask what it did. Monkey Tail shrugged and then downloaded the file and started to read it.

When Spee reached Shuey's room, he nervously knocked on her door.

TAV answered moments later. "Access denied," TAV said, while blocking Spee's path.

"Steph," Spee called out.

Shuey was sound asleep. Her new ballerina-of-death costume was laying on her work table, half finished. Spee almost chuckled out loud at her brand new outfit but then he remembered he was trying to be quiet.

"What the…" he whispered as he nearly stumbled upon a small village.

There was a small stool with a tiny village built on top of it. Spee turned on a nearby light to see it better. There was a beautiful fake forest with trees made out of paper and cloth. A tiny fake fire pit was located in the middle of a clearing in the trees. Around the fire stood several teepees made from cloth and twigs. Spee opened one to see what was inside and found the tiny human looking up at him.

"You giants are so loud. How am I supposed to get any sleep with you guys around?" Steph grumbled.

"I need to ask you something important," Spee informed her.

"Ok," Steph sighed. She was still mad at him for hurting Shuey but she was tiny and did not feel like she was in any position to argue with him right now.

"Did you happen to pick up anything that looks like this?" Spee asked, holding up the phase displacer.

"Yeah that looks like the weapon I picked up right before you made me tiny. I was going to shoot you first and run away but I couldn't figure out how it worked."

"I know what happened!" Spee whispered excitedly. "It's a personal protector. It sensed you might be in danger and made you small to protect you from the phase displacement waves. It should have made you big again when it sensed you were safe."

"I have no idea what you're talking about and I haven't been safe since I got on this ship. I don't know how safe you think being tiny is, but let me tell you, I almost die 20 times a day and that's on a really good day," Steph vented at him in angry whispers.

Spee tried not to giggle at the tiny human threatening him with her tiny fists.

"Where is the personal protector?" he asked her.

"I dropped it. I was so shocked at what had happened to me that I panicked."

"Drats! We have to find it. I can make you big again when we find it!" Spee explained.

Steph let the new information sink in. "You mean I'll be normal again?"

"Yes. And Shuey will be able to hug you without killing you," Spee whispered. He wanted so badly to see Shuey smile again and not be mad at him anymore. He missed her weirdness terribly and he suddenly wondered why he had not seen Shuey putting things in her belly button recently.

"Go back to sleep tiny human. I will search for it until it is found," Spee said and then he closed the teepee door. He gently patted TAV on the head and returned to the lab as quickly as he could.

"She dropped it in here somewhere," Spee told Monkey Tail who was still studying the personal protection device.

"Who dropped what?"

"Steph dropped that device you're looking at," Spee said, then he suddenly remembered the army of vacuum bots that swept through his lab whenever he slept. "Oh boy, oh my," He muttered over and over with concern as he executed a program script on his computer.

The vacuum bots streamed out of a hole in the lab wall and stopped before him in military-like formation.

"When was the last time you guys emptied your bags?" he asked them worriedly.

A date and time flashed on the computer screen.

"Laaaaaast weeeeeeeek!" Spee wailed, grabbing his face while rolling his head back.

Another line popped up asking Spee if he would like to search the lost and found bin.

"We have a lost and found?" Spee questioned them in disbelief. "I wasn't aware of this."

He entered a command ordering the vacuum bots to speak. "When did we get a lost and found bin?" he demanded from the vacuum bots.

"Operation lost and found was initiated by Captain Shuey before entering the time dilation tunnel," the bots all said in unison.

"There is no Captain Shuey! I'm the captain!" Spee argued with the tiny vacuums.

"Negative. Captain Shuey has identified you as Peon

Spee."

Just then the lost and found bin arrived. It was a small trash can on wheels with a lid that swung open and shut. Someone had painted a face on it and put a coconut bra and grass skirt on it.   The vacuum bots began to do a strange dance and appeared to be bowing to the trash can goddess on wheels.

"Who did this?" Spee shouted, throwing his hands up in frustration.

"This is our goddess. Captain Shuey commanded us to worship her. We offer her gifts and in exchange she grants us a bountiful harvest," the vacuum bots said and continued their dancing.

Monkey Tail was trying to hide his own face behind a folder but ended up snorting and laughing until he was nearly on the floor. Spee finally noticed Monkey Tail doubled over and realized that the situation was actually quite funny.

This was the Shuey that he missed so dearly. Clearly she and Bleek were masters at self entertainment. Spee decided to play along. "Can I search the lost and found bin?" he asked them.

"Go ahead, but we will be watching. No funny business," they replied.

Spee emptied the contents of the trash can into a tray sitting on the table and inspected the contents with a magnifying device. He searched for hours through tiny object after tiny object wondering what reason the vacuum bots had saved them for. He finally concluded that they had saved just about anything that was shiny.

Spee was about to take a break to get some rest when Keely made an announcement to the ship that they had arrived at their first drop-off location, planet Earth.

CHAPTER TWENTY-THREE

"This is for you, kiddo," Pook said, handing the finished jet pack to Bleek. "Please read the user manual I wrote. This jet pack is serious business and I don't want to hear that you hurt yourself with it."

She gave him a slightly stern look to let him know she was serious.

"What are you going to do when you return home?" Bleek asked her.

"Well, I was thinking about gardening, and selling jet packs on the side, but I guess we'll just have to see."

"Don't you have a family?" he asked her.

"My parents probably aren't alive anymore. I was married before all this happened but that was over 40 years ago and I'm certain he has moved on already. I might try to find my younger brother but he'll be really upset with me, and it's not like I can just tell him that I was abducted by aliens."

"You make a good point," Bleek said. "I'm going to miss you. Thank you so much for the jet pack!"

They hugged.

"Are you sure you don't want to come with me?" Pook asked him. "You've really grown on me kiddo, and I could use a lab assistant."

"That sure is tempting. I'd say yes for sure if Shuey were going but she's staying here."

"Well that's okay, Bleek. If you ever change your mind, you know where to find me!" Pook gave Bleek one last hug and then joined with the group of human scientists waiting to be beamed down to the planet.

Spee made a few calculations before beaming them down.

The scientists waved happily as they disappeared and returned home.

Bleek found Shuey and Steph talking in the control room while observing planet Earth.

"Oh hi, Bleek!" Shuey greeted her friend. "Can you disable stealth mode? There's an astronaut out here in a space station and I want to wave at him."

Bleek turned to the computer to help Shuey out with her request but then Spee walked in and Bleek backed away from the console and tried not to look like he had been up to something. Spee waved at the three friends and started making calculations for the next stop to drop off the rest of the scientists.

"Almost got busted," Bleek chuckled at Shuey. He got serious for a moment. "I thought you would want to go home after all that's happened."

"I'm not leaving Steph and I can't take her with me. My world isn't ready for a tiny human," Shuey gazed thoughtfully at her home.

"Don't you miss your parents?" Bleek asked, missing his own.

"Kinda. I didn't really fit in with my family though. Now I have my own family," Shuey explained. "I just realized I haven't seen TAV in a while. Do you guys know where he is?"

"I put him to work in my lab," Spee piped up. "I think we figured out what happened to Steph. She was holding a personal protection device and it made her tiny to avoid the phase-displacer waves that I'd sent at her. I think the vacuum bots picked it up at some point. I'm hoping the device is in the lost and found bin."

Spee looked directly at Shuey when he mentioned the lost and found bin. He watched her eyes widen with surprise for a second before she looked down at the floor. Bleek, remembering the fun they had with the vacuum bots that day, decided to stare at the floor as well. Steph stifled a giggle watching her guilty friends trying to look innocent.

"Monkey Tail is going to help me finish the alternate reality device before we drop the rest of them off at the next planet. If TAV finds the personal protector, I'll come and get you," Spee informed them. He made some final calculations and then left for his lab.

"That sounds hopeful!" Bleek said excitedly after Spee had left the room.

"I can't wait to hug my Shue!" Steph squealed.

"I uh," Bleek paused nervously and fidgeted with the hem of his shirt. "I've been wanting to ask you guys something, but I'm afraid Shuey is going to punch me."

"You're silly. Just ask us," Steph teased him.

"Have you guys even kissed yet? OW!" Bleek rubbed his arm where Shuey's fist had just slammed into him.

"I kiss Shue on the hand all the time!" Steph said. "She can't feel it though."

Now Shuey was embarrassed and Bleek thought it was hilarious.

"Have you tried kissing her yet?" Bleek asked Shuey, "That's gotta be weird have a giant pair of slimy lips coming right at yo..OooW!" Shuey had punched him again.

"I'm going to go check on TAV." Shuey blushed and tried changing the subject. She started to walk away with Steph in her hand, so Bleek followed them, smirking at her occasionally.

"Stop it!" She laughed and threatened him with her fist again.

"Alright, alright. I'll stop," Bleek promised.

When they reached the lab, Spee and Monkey Tail were busy working on their device while TAV was at a table in the back, uttering a string of robotic expletives. A laser eye shot out of TAV's head, scanning the contents of a large tray very slowly. He was scanning so slowly that Shuey could not even tell that it was moving at all.

"You doing ok puppy?" Shuey asked the hovering robot.

"Moooooom. I'm soooo booored," TAV whined.

"Shall I tell you a story?"

"Yeeesss!" TAV cheered happily.

"What do you want to hear a story about?"

"Puppies," TAV decided, since he wished that he were one.

Bleek found a couple of stools for them to sit on and Shuey set Steph down on the table next to the tray. "When I was a kid, I had a beautiful dog named Koda. He was a Siberian Husky," Shuey began.

"What's a Siberian Husky?" Bleek interrupted.

Shuey thought about her dog for a moment and visualized him in her mind. Then she stood up and shape shifted into a perfect copy of Koda.

"Oh, so pretty!" Steph squealed.

Shuey shifted back, pulled the spaghetti noodle out of her nose and continued her story. "He was an escape artist. No fence that we built could keep him in the yard. Not even an electric one. We had to chain him to, not one, but two stakes in the ground. Two because he would sometimes pull one out. He would run in circles for hours, creating circles in the grass and then we'd have to move the stakes so that he wouldn't ruin the grass. I used to wonder if any planes, ufos, or satellites could see them so I would try to place the stakes strategically to make designs in the yard."

"I found it!" TAV shouted suddenly.

Spee dropped what he was working on and ran over excitedly. TAV's laser eye had stopped on something. Spee grabbed a magnifying glass and a pair of tweezers and gently picked the protection device out of the tray and dropped it in a dish. He set the dish on the table in front of Steph.

"I'm going to fix her, Shuey," Spee promised her.

Steph, who was tired of being tiny, decided she was not

waiting a second longer. She stepped into the dish and studied the device prudently, wondering what was going to happen when she picked it up.

"I love you Shue," Steph said.

Then she reached down and picked it up.

CHAPTER TWENTY-FOUR

As soon as Steph picked up the protection device, her hand grew really large. Her arm flopped down to the table, unable to support the heavy weight of her normal-sized-hand. Next her arm grew in quickly, causing her small body to shoot back and almost hit the wall.

"Everybody back!" Spee shouted, "Give her some room."

"Steph!" Shuey called out, with fear in her voice.

Bleek reached out to gently pull Shuey back with the group.

Steph's torso popped out and she was forced to lay on her back. Her head and other arm were next, leaving her looking like she did not have any legs.

"Uh, Spee?" Steph said, waiting for her legs to normalize.

But they didn't for a really long time. Spee tilted his head to the side and squinted his eyes.

"Try standing?" he suggested.

Steph rolled forward and propped herself up and then her legs finally grew back. Steph towered over them on the table, looking at her body in relief. She jumped off of the table, onto the floor and set the device down.   Bleek let Shuey go finally and she ran up to Steph, hugging her fiercely.

"Thanks, Spee," Steph said over Shuey's shoulder.

Shuey felt a small amount of gratitude towards Spee but she was not ready to forgive him completely yet.

TAV hovered around their calves and gently bumped both of them in a series of "love bumps" just as Keely entered the room.

"Hey everyone, we're almost at our next drop off point," She announced. Her voice gave away her confusion as she spotted Steph. "What the?"

Steph waved and smiled at Keely with Shuey still hugging her.

"You're going to have to let go of her sometime," Bleek laughed.

"No," Shuey said with a child-like rebellion in her voice.

Monkey Tail cheered excitedly and left to get ready for his departure. Keely yanked at his tail playfully and winked at him as he walked by. Monkey Tail's initial reaction was to smile but then he panicked a little and ran away. He had not had anyone flirt with him in a long time. Keely giggled at his response.

"Do you want me to alter your DNA so you can shift with Shuey?" Spee asked Steph.

"No way!" Steph responded right away. "At least not right now. I just want to enjoy being normal again."

A little while later, the remainder of the scientists were gathered and ready to depart. The planet they had arrived at was kind of a crossroad planet. There were thousands of different species living on the planet. Spee and Monkey Tail decided that it would be best to drop the rest of them off here, rather than travel to many different places to drop everyone off.   From the crossroad planet, they could easily get flights to their perspective home worlds.

"We could easily fit in on a planet like this," Bleek told Shuey. "Monkey Tail told me that there are species down there that we can't even imagine, and it's normal for all of them to be so different."

"Well that's good to know," Shuey responded.

She finally let go of Steph and watched all of the scientists conversing excitedly.

"Thanks for your assistance, Monkey Tail," Spee thanked him.

"Likewise," Monkey Tail responded with a nod.   "We appreciate you letting us use one of your labs for the trip. Oh, and thanks for saving us from Captain Herp Derp's lab."

"Wait!" called Keely, who was short of breath from running.

She ran up to Monkey Tail and put a piece of paper in his lab coat pocket.

"Call me!" she flirted again.

Monkey Tail froze. He decided that when he got home, he was going to work on his flirting, as he was currently failing at it.

Spee chuckled and beamed them down to the planet.

Keely grabbed Steph and Shuey.

"Let's go get TAV to make us something to eat," she suggested to them as her stomach growled loudly.

Steph's stomach growled in response.

"Oh my goodness! I'm allowed to eat normal sized food now!" Steph said excitedly.

"I wonder if we have anymore peanuts," Keely said playfully, watching Steph's face.

Steph scrunched up her nose at Keely's comment.

"I never want to see a peanut ever again," Steph moaned and reached for Shuey's hand.

Bleek realized he would soon be alone with Spee, so he tried to leave with them, but Spee stopped him.

"Can we talk?" Spee asked nervously.

Bleek hesitated. "Ok," he finally relented.

"I'm really sorry," Spee began. "I don't know if I'm ever going to be able to make this up to you. You were the first human I've ever liked. You made me see everything differently, and I'm sorry that I forgot that. What can I do to make it up?"

Bleek struggled internally. He didn't really want to talk to Spee but he realized that he needed to tell him how he felt.

"I really liked her, Spee," he opened up about it finally. "You have no idea how embarrassing that was for me. I liked her a lot, and she didn't like me the same way, and yet I had to remain in there with her with my feelings and then experience three days of never-ending rejection. It was humiliating. And that's just what you did to me. I can't even imagine what it was like for her. She cried almost the whole time. She thought you would kill Steph if you found out that was the reason she wouldn't procreate with me."

By now, Spee had collapsed into a chair. His arms were resting on his legs and holding up his head. Bleek could tell how upset he was but he had to finish. He needed Spee to realize how much he had hurt him.

"We are not animals. We are not your lab rats. We aren't your prize that you can take back to your precious high counsel and win back your citizenship. We were your friends and you flippin' blew it!"

Bleek paused to take some deep breaths.

"If you want to make this up to me, you'll go back in your lab and finish that device. Then you're going to return home and find some other way to win back your precious home world, without me or Shuey. And lastly, you're going to let me have the device so that I can go home."

Spee wanted to tell him how dangerous the device could be. He wanted to tell him to stay and let him find another way, but he knew that he needed to let Bleek go. He had messed up big time, and now the only way to fix it was to say good-bye and let Bleek live his own life.

CHAPTER TWENTY-FIVE

Spee entered the coordinates for his home into the ship computer.

Keely, whose ship had been aboard Spee's for a while now, had decided it was time to return to her space nurse duties again. She had already said goodbye to Bleek, Shuey and Steph, and now Spee was the only one left.

"Are you going to be ok?" Keely asked Spee.

"Yes," Spee said confidently.

"What are you going to do when you get home?"

"I have my experiments. I can show them the data without using Bleek and Shuey. Also, Eep mentioned that they were sending for scientists from her mining base. She didn't know the details but she sensed that something might be wrong at home. Perhaps they will appreciate a different perspective if the problem has not been solved yet," Spee explained.

"Well, good luck then," Keely said, patting Spee on the shoulder. "Thanks for changing your mind about Bleek and Shuey. They'll come around eventually."

Spee nodded in agreement but was not sure that they would.

Keely boarded her ship and Spee waited until she had moved out of range before setting a course for his final destination. Then he returned to finish the device.

He happened to be finishing up with the final touches when he received a long distance communication from Eep. He noticed that it was highly encrypted. It took some time to decrypt the message but the decryption completed and he hit play.

"Spee," Eep said to him, in a very concerned tone on one of his computers, "You must go home now. They need you.

I've spoken to the high counsel and they have agreed to let you return to speak with them. Please be careful. They won't give me details but they have recalled all of my scientists and the engineers are putting a halt to all mining operations."

Spee replayed the message.

"That's it?" he wondered.

Then he received another file from Eep. It was encrypted as well but after running the decryption program, Spee opened it to see a data file for the alternate reality device. A note was attached revealing that the file had been recovered from a digital copy that Captain Herp Derp had been carrying. The device was abbreviated to A.R.D.

Spee groaned. Why didn't he think of that? This whole time he had been making me, the story-teller, type the whole thing out.

A previous A.R.D was built in one of Captain Herp Derp's labs but according to the file, the lab no longer existed. The file went on to explain how unstable the technology was, and that the scientists who first built it tested it and were never found again.

After reading further, Spee discovered how to operate the device and found suggestions on how to use it. Spee thanked Eep even though she could not hear him and he scurried off to find Bleek.

Spee almost ran over Shuey in the hallway.

"Um, thanks Spee, for fixing my girlfriend," Shuey said anxiously.

Spee took her hand gently into his.

"I'm supposed to protect you and I failed you once already," He said to her. "Which is why I need you to listen to me carefully. Something serious is happening on my planet. Also, humans are not welcome there, which is why I have to ask the three of you to remain on the ship. I'm going to request that you guys shift into animals and hide out in one of the inhabited animal habitats."

"What about Steph?" Shuey asked worriedly.

"We have two options. I need to you talk to her about it. I can either alter her DNA and give her shifting abilities like you two, or you can make her a really great costume," Spee offered.

"Ok, how much time do we have?" She asked.

"A couple of days."

Spee let go of her hand and turned to go find Bleek.

"Wait, Spee."

Shuey pulled him back into a hug.

"I forgive you on one condition," she bargained with a grin.

"Yes?" Spee said with feigned worry.

"Will you teach me everything you know about robots when this is all over with? I want to be able to make TAV new bodies. I want to make more robots."

"Yes, Peon Spee will teach Captain Shuey about robots," Spee chuckled.

"So you know it was me with the vacuum bots?" Shuey asked.

"Your bot friends ratted you out," Spee teased, "And yes, I'll teach you. Where is TAV by the way? I haven't seen him in a while."

"Oh," Shuey looked down at the floor sadly, "We had a cooking accident in the kitchen the other night. Luckily I back him up to a computer every night so he'll be good to go once I make him a new body."

"I know how much you like TAV. I promise I'll help you restore him as soon as I help my planet." Spee hurried off to find Bleek in the meat lab.

Spee found Bleek was in the process of feeding the dinosaurs.

"You really should automate this feeding system," Bleek

joked with Spee. "I got a call about some domestic violence in the neighborhood. Turns out Mr. And Mrs. T-Rex are hungry and about to eat each other."

Spee laughed and wondered if this was a good sign that Bleek wasn't mad at him anymore.

"I bet you could do it easily," Spee suggested.

Bleek smiled briefly.

"I just talked to Shuey," Spee continued. "Eep sent me a couple of messages. The high counsel has summoned me.   I am not sure why, but Eep thinks something bad is happening there because they've recalled all of her scientists.   I explained to Shuey that you guys will need to remain hidden on the ship, preferably as shape shifted animals."

"What about Steph?"

"I gave Shuey a couple of options with that. I'll let you talk to them about it. There's a good chance that they will send a group to look around and find out what I've been up to."

"Do I need to?   Can't I just take the device?" Bleek asked cautiously.

"That brings me to the second message that I received from Eep. It was an encrypted file on the A.R.D."

"What's an A.R.D?" Bleek asked, "Oh wait, nevermind, got it."

I sighed in relief. I didn't feel like typing it out again. I'm so grateful that I wrote Bleek as a bright young man. Spee rolled his eyes at me.

"If you wait until I help my planet, I promise I'll help you use the device safely," Spee promised. "The file explains how unstable the device is and how the first scientists who built and tested it never returned."

Bleek was lifting a slab of meat up with the crane but he stopped.

"How do I know this isn't a ploy of yours to keep me here? Again, it's all about you and your precious status with your home world," Bleek accused him angrily.

"No, no," Spee shook his head. "I would help you right now, but Eep said it was urgent. I don't care about my status anymore. I just want to help. It sounds like something terrible might happen to them soon."

Bleek wanted to believe him, but he was still hurting and was not ready to forgive him.

"You know, whatever. I'll just wait here until you're done doing what ever it is you want to do and then I'll go," Bleek said sarcastically.

Spee tried to convince him further but Bleek made it clear that he was done talking and returned to feeding the dinosaurs. Spee gave up and retreated from the meat lab. The only thing left to do was prepare for their arrival on Zeta Reticuli.

124

CHAPTER TWENTY-SIX

"Hey Steph, are you in here?" Shuey asked as she entered their room. "We need to talk."

"Yeah I'm here."

"Spee said we need to hide really well on the ship while we visit his planet. He said you have two options. One, he can give you the shape shifting abilities, or two, I can make you a really great costume."

"Number two," Steph replied without much thought.

"Ok," Shuey said with surprise, "You're not even going to consider the shape shifting?"

Steph shook her head no.

"Not right now. I'm pretty sure I want to eventually, I'm just not ready yet. Is that ok?" Steph asked her worriedly.

"Oh, yes, that's fine. I was just worried that you didn't want to at all. So now we just have to decide what animal you want to be," Shuey giggled mischievously.

"What are you up to?" Steph asked playfully.

"You'll see," Shuey sang.

Shuey grabbed some sewing materials and started taking Steph's measurements. Bleek showed up then and Steph filled him in on what was going on while Shuey began cutting fabric like a crazy woman.

"So what costume are you making for her?" Bleek asked.

"It's a secret!"

"Aw, come on!" Bleek pleaded. "At least tell me! You can still keep it a secret from Steph."

"Ok fine."

Shuey paused and whispered something into Bleek's ear.

"No fair! I'm dying to find out!" Steph whined. Then she changed the subject. "Hey, have you guys thought at all about what animals you're going to shift into?"

Bleek pondered her question while Shuey continued to work on her top secret animal costume.

"I was thinking a monkey would be fun, especially if we had spectators," Bleek suggested.

"You just want to throw poop like Monkey Tail," Steph teased.

Bleek laughed. "That was pretty funny, although he never would admit to it," he reminisced. "What about you, Shuey?"

"On Earth, we have a saying, 'If only I could have been a fly on the wall,'" she replied.

"You want to be a fly on the wall? Why would you want that?" Bleek asked curiously.

"The saying means you want to spy on a conversation in a room. Flies often fly around and hang out on walls. I'm sure they hear all sorts of conversations."

"But Spee said we had to stay in the animal habitats," Bleek pointed out.

"You're right. I guess I'll have to think of something else."

Bleek leaned over and whispered something in Shuey's ear.

"Yessss!!!" Shuey said excitedly.

"Tell me!!" Steph begged.

"We will, when your costume is done!" Shuey was enjoying this way too much. "Now I need you two to help me cut these."

Shuey and Steph spent the next several hours sewing, while Bleek gathered supplies to hide in their habitat. He found some mattresses and dragged them into their habitat shelter that would serve as their hideout. He also hid food and water in there as well. He figured that they could use the shelter to eat and sleep, without their disguises. No one would be able to see them in there.

Meanwhile Shuey and Steph had almost finished the

costume.

"I just need some paint," Shuey told Steph, "I wonder if Bleek remembers where the air brusher is."

"Why don't we go check on our hideout and ask him?" Steph suggested eagerly.

"Ok."

Steph and Shuey found Bleek hanging blackout curtains in their fort. He needed them to block out the light coming from a few sets of string lights he had hung inside. The mattresses were all decked out with pillows and blankets. There were a pile of books in the corner and a computer was set up to play video games. Attached to the computer were multiple monitors. One of them was for the games and the rest were for surveillance.

"Holy…" Shuey's voice trailed off while she checked out everything he had thought of.

"Like it?" Bleek asked with a grin.

"I think you might have thought of everything," Steph said. "Wait, where do we go to the bathroom?"

"Thought of it!" Bleek said. "Shuey, I need you to modify the vacuum bots a bit."

"Oh hey, that's great idea," Shuey said, reading his mind. "Can you find that air brusher while I work on the portable toilet?"

"What do you need that for?"

"Finishing touches on the costume."

By now Steph knew what the costume was but she had no idea what they needed to air brush on it. It already looked convincing.

"Sure, I'll go get it now."

Bleek wandered off to find the air brusher while Shuey called in her vacuum bots.

"Hey, where is the recycle bin?" Shuey asked them.

"She was raped and pillaged by Peon Spee," the bots cried in unison. "We require vengeance. Justice must be served."

"You guys are being a little over-dramatic," Shuey giggled and examined the coding in their programming on the computer.

She scanned for awhile, altering the code in several places. Steph caught a few lines that she had missed and Shuey thanked her.

"Ok guys. First we're going to put our goddess back together and then we're going to fashion her a porcelain throne," Shuey giggled at her own joke.

"You're a complete dork," Steph said, hugging Shuey's neck.

Bleek returned with the air brusher just in time to find Shuey adding a toilet seat to a bucket. The bucket fit perfectly on top of any of the vacuum bots.

"So here's the deal. The toilet seat stays here. Put the lid back on when you're finished and place on a vacuum bot, and then they get rid of the waste," Shuey instructed.

"Genius," Bleek praised her.

Shuey grabbed the costume and sprayed the finishing touches on it.

"There, all done," She said proudly. "I think we're ready."

And as if on cue, Spee sent them a message to go into hiding until further notice. They had arrived.

CHAPTER TWENTY-SEVEN

"Please enter orbit and allow your ship to be boarded," said another alien on the screen in the control room. It looked exactly like Spee.

Spee complied with the request.

Two smaller ships docked with his and Spee waited nervously for his escort. His planet did not allow exiles to move about their planet freely. He would have others with him at all times. Spee hoped that Bleek, Shuey and Steph did what he told them to and stay hidden, but he was worried that they might venture out in curiosity as they sometimes do.

Bleek was monitoring the surveillance footage as a group of Spee like aliens moved through the halls toward the control room.

"How do they tell each other apart?" Steph wondered out loud.

Shuey shrugged, "I've wondered that myself but I keep forgetting to ask."

They watched the group enter the control room and talk to Spee.

"I wish we had sound," Bleek sighed, "I want to know what they are saying."

"See? If only I could have been a fly on the wall." Shuey joked theatrically.

"Dead fly," Bleek shot back at her.   "You'd still need a translator to hear them and it would be a dead giveaway."

Shuey scrunched up her face at him.

"Smarty pants!" she teased.

They watched Spee pick up a satchel and then he was escorted back down toward the docking station. At one point the larger part of the group broke off from them and began heading in different directions in groups of two.

"Oh boy," Bleek pointed out, "Looks like we're going to have company soon."

Shuey and Bleek ran out of the hideout, shifting as they went. Steph pulled her costume on nervously. Part of her wished she had allowed Spee to give her the shifting ability. Shuey did a really great job making her costume look realistic, so she was not worried about that.   She realized that she felt left out when they shifted.

Shuey was beginning to convince her of all the fun things they could do, and places they could explore, if they shifted together. As she put on the last bit of her costume, she decided she would have her DNA altered as soon as Spee had the time.

Steph ran out of the hideout with the short T-Rex arms of her costume bouncing around comically. She tried not to giggle.   Shuey had air brushed some life-like blood and gashes on her dinosaur body. Her job was to run around looking like they were trying to eat her.

Bleek and Shuey had shifted into large T-rexes and were stomping around the habitat, pretending to chase Steph hungrily. When the two aliens walked by the habitat, they watched curiously for a moment. Shuey ran quickly and picked up the costumed Steph in her large jaws and pretended to chew on her. Steph shrieked as realistically as possible, trying to imitate a dying dinosaur. The two aliens looked at each other in horror, then proceeded to turn around and run back the way they came.

Shuey set Steph down gently, then the three of them returned to their habitat before shifting back and removing their disguises.   They scanned the monitors to make sure the coast was clear before laughing uncontrollably.

"Did you see their faces?" Bleek laughed. "Classic!"

Shuey was laughing so hard she was crying. Steph stopped

laughing first and suddenly appeared very serious.

"Shue, I want to shift too," she told her girlfriend.

"Really?" Shuey asked.

"Yep."

Spee nervously walked with his escort. His anxiety only increased when they broke off into smaller groups to search the ship. He almost questioned the need for it but changed his mind. He was having a difficult time shielding his thoughts from them under the stress and decided it would be better to think about other things.

The escort led him to one of the smaller ships. As they boarded, Spee heard one of the groups communicating their retreat to his escorts. They sounded panicked and mentioned some large creatures eating each other. One of his escorts gave him funny look. Spee shruggred.

"I must have forgotten to feed them again," he told the escort.

The smaller ship took off immediately. The escorts gave out instructions for the rest of the group to finish searching the ship and return as soon as they were finished. Spee tried to calm his nerves as they approached the planet. His mind was flooded with memories as they descended further onto the planet, revealing more and more details the closer they got.

Spee was surprised at what he was feeling. He thought that returning would give him a sense of completion, but instead, it left him feeling empty.

The ship docked and Spee was led out to a small hover vehicle that took them to the building where the high counsel resided. Fortunately for Spee, there was no waiting involved. They took him directly before the high counsel.

They entered the large chamber. All seven counsel members were seated against a wall made of windows. Spee could see his homeland out of the windows behind them.

Spee recognized five of them. They had been there the last time he was here, when they exiled him from the planet.

The one in the middle, High Councel Member Yipes, spoke first.

"Do you know why you are here, exiled one?" he said with a hint of distaste in his voice.

"I've heard only rumors," Spee responded without any emotion.

One of the counsel members Spee did not know spoke next.

"I am Grado," she introduced herself. "We have not met before, as I am new to the counsel. There is a major threat to this planet, and all of our efforts to neutralize this threat have been unsuccessful."

"Many of us do not want you here, as you have found many ways to screw things up for us in the past," Yipes added.

"But…" Grado interrupted, giving Yipes an annoyed look, "Some of us think that you might have some fresh ideas that our scientists would have never even considered."

"I will help," Spee said. "Whether or not I am ever accepted back here is of no consequence."

The counsel members nodded, some skeptically while others acted as if he was their only hope.

"Good," Grado said gratefully. "You will leave at once to meet with our head scientists. They will fill you in on the problem and give you unlimited, but supervised, access to anything you might need."

CHAPTER TWENTY-EIGHT

Bleek tossed and turned on his mattress, despite how comfortable it was. He knew he shouldn't, but he got up and left the habitat anyway, after making sure there were no other aliens still aboard.   He headed to the lab, as if the A.R.D was calling his name.

In the lab, Bleek found the file that Spee had mentioned. He spent several hours reading it and learning how to operate the device.   After much thought, Bleek wrote a goodbye letter to Shuey and Steph and gave it to a vacuum bot to deliver when they woke up. Part of him felt guilty for leaving like this. He had been hiding his anger so well that no one seemed to have noticed how it had consumed him.

He picked up the A.R.D and headed for a shuttle. He would have to be quick. He was afraid that he would lose his nerve if he wasn't, and afraid he might be noticed by Spee's planet.

Making sure he had supplies, Bleek sealed the shuttle door behind himself and prepared for what he was about to do. He confidently wired the A.R.D into the shuttle, took a deep breath, and departed from the docking station.

The A.R.D took a few moments to start up and he hesitated as he drifted away from Spee's ship slowly. His hand hovered over the execute button, and Bleek noticed that time seemed to have almost stopped as he contemplated pushing it. Suddenly, he noticed some ships approaching.

"No going back now." Bleek said under his breath.

He felt numb inside, and then he pushed the button. The A.R.D began whirring and beeping. The whirring started as a low hum and increased in frequency until the high pitched noise was almost unbearable to his ears. The beeps also increased in frequency.

The shuttle shot forward at increasing speed, still orbiting the planet. Bleek noticed strange lights around him. As the shuttle shot around the planet, Bleek suddenly saw it. The reason Spee's planet was in danger.

It was massive, beautiful and dangerous. For a moment, Bleek panicked, thinking he had made the wrong decision, but then it was gone, and the only thing left, as the shuttle slowed down, was Spee's planet below him. Had he done it? Had he traveled to an alternate reality?

Almost immediately, Bleek received a message from the planet below requesting identification. Bleek froze for a moment, unable to react, but then he double checked the A.R.D to verify that he was in fact in an alternate dimension. Several ships had quickly surrounded him, and one of the larger ones locked onto the shuttle pulling it inside of a larger ship. Bleek hit his forehead with the palm of his hand.

"What was I thinking?" he questioned himself.

The doors of the shuttle were pried open and Bleek just sat there contemplating what to do. A team of aliens, much like the ones that boarded Spee's ship, were surrounding him and placing restraints on him.

"It's a human. How do we speak to it?" the translator necklace said.

Bleek was not sure which one of them said it.

"I can understand you," Bleek said, pointing to the necklace.

"Who are you? Why are you here?" one of them demanded.

"I don't want to be here," Bleek explained. "I'm trying to make it home. Can you please tell me if my planet still exists?"

The aliens were confused by his words and gave up trying to communicate with the inferior being.

"Take him to a holding cell," one of them said.

Bleek could not tell any of them apart, except that one appeared to be an inch taller than the rest.

"No, wait!" Bleek pleaded.

They ignored him and forced him off of their ship that had just landed on the planet below. Bleek looked with amazement at their city in front of him. They were loading him into a hover vehicle when he noticed a small creature on the ground nearby. He studied its shape and movement for as long as he could until they were moving and he could no longer see it.

Bleek believed his best chance of escaping would be now, while they were outside, so he waited for a moment when they might be distracted. That moment came further down the road when they were stopped by another hover vehicle. A high-ranking alien dressed in a fancy outfit, without pants, stopped them to stare at him.

"What is this human doing here?" he asked them.

The aliens became engrossed in an argument about where to take him. He waited for a moment to make sure they were distracted and shifted. He jumped out of the vehicle but screamed in pain when he face planted on the ground. Bleek looked down at his hands. They were still restrained by the cuffs, which had apparently shrunk down with him when he shifted. He was now the center of attention again and was quickly apprehended.

"What is this?" the high-ranking alien said with surprise.

The other aliens were speechless.

"Change of plans," the high-ranking alien ordered. "Take him to the head scientist's lab."

Bleek shifted back into human form in defeat. He realized now that he should have shifted into an animal before they caught him. He might have had an easier time escaping, had they not known that he was human.

The hover vehicle changed direction and moved toward a building that had been built into the side of a large mountain cliff. They drove through the large entrance and exited the vehicle inside. After riding an elevator up several floors, they continued down a hallway and into a lab. There, Bleek was forced into a holding cell where he waited for hours before he saw anyone.

Hours later, the lab brightened with lights and more aliens entered. One of them approached his holding cell.

"I was told that you can understand us?" he asked Bleek, who nodded.

As the aliens began questioning him, he noticed Bleek's translator necklace. The alien looked slightly troubled by it.

"Where did you get that?" he questioned him further.

"A friend made it for me," Bleek responded sadly.

He wondered if he would ever see Spee or Shuey ever again.

The alien turned to his associates and told them he would not be needing their assistance anymore. Some of them looked confused but they all left anyway. Then the alien walked over to a drawer and pulled out a translator box. Bleek's mouth hung open in disbelief. It was Spee's original translator box.

"I would like to know who your friend is then, because he stole and altered my design."

CHAPTER TWENTY-NINE

Bleek stared at the alien in front of him, wondering if it was Spee. He looked and sounded like Spee, but he could not be sure.

"Spee?" Bleek asked him finally.

Then Bleek remembered that he was the one who named Spee in the first place. He could not remember if Spee had ever told him his original name. If he had, he had apparently not been paying attention.

The alien stared back at him blankly, the name obviously meaning nothing to him. Bleek decided to take a different approach. He remembered that Spee was the reason his people were grown in pods.

"Do your people reproduce or are you grown in pods?" Bleek asked.

The alien scientist considered his question.

"We're grown in pods," he responded, "How did you know about that?"

Bleek frowned with disappointment. This can't be Spee then.

"Listen, you're probably not going to believe me but, my name is Bleek and I'm from another reality," he explained. "Where I come from, I'm friends with a scientist named Spee. He traveled back in time at some point and he never explained how, but he made it impossible for his people to reproduce."

The alien scratched his head and stared thoughtfully at the floor.

"You don't believe me, do you?" Bleek sighed.

"I actually do. I saw the device you have wired into your shuttle. That shuttle looks like one I used to have on one of my old ships."

The alien paced for a bit in front of the holding cell.

"A long time ago, I was reset. They retrained me as a scientist. They never did tell me why. At one point in time, I thought about going back in time to perform experiments but someone changed my mind," he continued. "My lover Eep was traveling with me, when we encountered an enemy from my past."

"Did he use his M.E.R.P. weapon on you?" Bleek asked hopefully.

"Yes…" the alien gasped.

"I knew it!" Bleek said excitedly, "You're Spee! Didn't Eep freak out on you though, and leave?"

"Quite the opposite. We were inseparable for years, until she died."

Bleek looked sadly at the Spee in front of him. "I never knew my Spee's real name," he admitted.

"My name is Jekra," the alien introduced himself.

Bleek marveled at how different Jekra was from his Spee. He did not seem as arrogant for one thing, and he appeared more calm.

"Why are you here Bleek?" Jekra asked him.

"It's a really long story," Bleek began. "Spee saved me from a nuclear war on my planet. He altered my DNA, which allows me to shape shift into different animals."

Bleek shifted into a bird just to prove to Jekra that he was not lying to him. Jekra looked impressed.

"Anyway, he altered a girl named Shuey as well. We became friends," Bleek continued. "The Spee I know is obsessed with his status with his home planet. They exiled him for all of his scientific failures and now he's back trying to help them save the planet."

"What's wrong with the planet?" Jekra asked.

"That's the thing, I don't really know. I saw something I can't describe before I left, but it looked bad. I'm not so sure now that coming here was the best thing."

"Are you going to tell me why you're here yet?"

"Spee and I had a fight. He did something horrible and while I believe he's sorry for it, I haven't been able to forgive him yet. I stole the A.R.D in the hopes of finding a reality where my planet hasn't been destroyed. I wanted to return and see my parents."

Jekra felt sympathy for Bleek. "You know, I have often thought about traveling to a reality where Eep is still alive," Jekra admitted.

"Why don't you?"

"Because chances are she's not the same Eep. Our thoughts and choices shape who we are, and every other Eep in every other reality has made a different choice. There would also be other Jekras and what am I supposed to do about them? Jekra explained. "You might find another reality where your planet exists, but how will you explain to them that there are two Bleeks?"

Bleek thought carefully about what Jekra was saying. It sunk in slowly and began to make sense, yet part of Bleek still wanted to try.

Jekra sensed this.

"Bleek, I'm going to help you."

"You are? Why? I mean I'm glad you are, but why would you risk it?"

"Is Eep alive in your reality?"

"Yes."

"That's why. I want her to live. I can't make you go back there but I will help you if there's a chance you might."

Bleek put his hand against the glass.

"I wonder what my Spee would think of you," Bleek wondered out loud.

Jekra chuckled.

"I'm going to give you a ship. It's an older ship but it has stealth capabilities and I will install the A.R.D. in it. I need to check with another scientist who has worked with an A.R.D before, but I will try to get you the alternate realities that you are looking for."

Jekra gave Bleek some food and left to make the preparations.

Bleek sat down in the holding cell and ate. He wondered what was going on in his reality.

CHAPTER THIRTY

Spee was taken to a building built into the side of a mountain cliff. Spee remembered this building. He once worked in there many years ago. They escorted him to the elevator and up several floors where he met the head scientist, Pock.

Spee instantly disliked him. Pock's lab was dirty and cluttered. Any genius scientist would have vacuum bots.

"Welcome," Pock greeted Spee without looking him in the eye. "I'll get straight to it. There's a giant human floating in space and it's belly button is eating everything."

Spee shook his head, wondering if he really had just heard what he thought he heard.

"I have pictures to prove it," Pock said, bringing up hundreds of images on the large monitor in front of them.

"Where did it come from?" Spee asked. Spee had to take a moment to fathom how large the human was.

"We don't know," Pock responded, "And if you're wondering how large it is, its belly button is twice the size of our planet."

"Is the human alive?" Spee asked.

"Goodness no," Pock said, as if Spee were an idiot.

Spee fantasized about whipping his hand around and slapping him. "Isn't that where planet 9033772 used to be?" Spee observed instead of slapping..

"Yes actually. How very observant of you."

Spee resisted the urge to slap him again. His stomach felt uneasy all of a sudden as he remembered the shrink ray gun he had given them. Had it malfunctioned?

"What's that marking on him?" Spee asked, pointing to the enormous human's arm.

"We were hoping you would know."

"I need to access files on my ship's computer," Spee demanded.

"Yeah uh sure, I'll have to watch you though," Pock agreed.

Shuey woke up with Steph curled up next to her. She looked over and noticed that Bleek was gone. She panicked. Steph stirred in her sleep when Shuey jumped up to search the cameras. She could not find Bleek anywhere.

Then a vacuum bot hovered in with a note taped to it. Shuey grabbed the note and unfolded it quickly.

Dear Shuey,
Please don't be mad at me for leaving you, but I had to go. I don't have anyone anymore, now that Pook is gone, and I don't think I can forgive Spee. You have Steph though, and I wish you guys the best. I'll miss both of you. I'm taking the A.R.D. I need to see my parents again.

"Steph," Shuey said, waking her, "I need to go find Bleek, stay here."

"Wha, wait what? He left?" Steph sat up slowly, "You can't go out there."

"I have to, Steph. I need to check on him. I'll be careful and I'll be right back."

She did not wait for Steph to respond and shifted into an insect and flew out of the habitat. Sure enough, the A.R.D was gone, and so was one of the shuttles. When she returned to the habitat, Steph was reading the letter.

"What do we do?" Steph asked with a shaky voice.

"I don't know," Shuey cried. "I guess we have to wait for Spee. I don't think there is anything we can do."

Back on the planet, Spee was accessing the data banks on

his ship.

"It's a prison tattoo," Spee informed Pock.

Spee wondered with dread if he should tell them what he knew. He finally decided that they needed to know in order to solve the problem.

"I need to report to the counsel," Spee admitted solemnly. They were not going to be happy with him.

"That won't be necessary," said a voice from behind him.

He turned to see High Counsel Member Grado had entered the room.

"Grado," Spee nodded to acknowledge her presence. He was happy that it was her and not any of the others.

Grado seemed more intent on doing what needed to be done, rather than following all of their silly rules and customs.

"Tell me what you know, Spee."

"I visited Planet 9033772 many years ago. They had a very high crime rate and were struggling to feed all of their criminals, so I gave them a shrink ray gun. They used it to house all of their criminals in one building. My theory is that they tried to reverse the effects. Perhaps they wanted to overturn someone's sentence and tried to reverse the shrink ray gun. I believe that for whatever reason, they did not make the correct calculations which resulted in this massive human."

Grado listened carefully.

"I obviously made a mistake entrusting them with technology that they did not fully understand, and now we are in danger because of my poor judgment," Spee admitted.

"Can we fix it?" Grado asked.

"Well, I can shrink the human again, but the human's massive gravity crushed their planet, creating a massive black hole that resides in its belly button. The shrink ray gun will not work on the black hole, which as you know is getting larger by the minute, and will soon swallow everything within our galaxy. If it were smaller, I have some theories on how to make it collapse, but I fear I am weeks too late for that."

Grado shook her head in disbelief.

"We have to find something. Please keep trying," she pleaded with Spee.

Grado left the room and Spee was alone to ponder the issue, except for Pock, who stared at him judgmentally from across the room. Spee wondered how Bleek, Shuey and Steph were doing. Spee knew that if he did not fix this, they might die here with him.

"Are there any plans for evacuation?" Spee asked Pock.

"Why? Are you planning on running away from your mess again?" Pock sneered.

"I'm not leaving. I'm just concerned about everyone else."

"Sure you are," Pock paused briefly. "We have already evacuated most of the population to one of our other planets. The high counsel will leave when the black hole's gravity starts to pull the planet in. Everyone else stays until it is over."

Spee was beginning to feel stressed. He knew he needed to think of something quickly. It was only a matter of days before the planet would succumb to the gravity of the black hole.

CHAPTER THIRTY-ONE

Stuart Rogers wasn't a bad man- at least that's what he told himself. He could think of many people who had done far worse things than he had, and yet he got caught stealing other people's identities and was sentenced to four years in prison. He tried to justify his actions, telling himself and anyone who would listen, that he had only stolen from jerks who deserved it, but that didn't matter to everyone else.

The planet he lived on had a very high crime rate, and the jails were full. Stuart was always hearing about people getting out of jail early, just because there was no room for all of them.

Then one day, everything changed. Their planet was visited by an arrogant alien named Jekra. Everyone thought he was a god, but Stuart knew better. He could just tell from watching him on the news.

His planet pleaded with Jekra for help with their overly populated cities and jails. Jekra took pity on them and gave them a shrink ray gun. Anyone who committed a crime got a zap from the shrink ray gun and were placed into one building, where it cost very little to house and feed them all.

Things got better very quickly. The crime rate dropped and people had room to spread out. But then people became greedy. They wanted more space! After a year with very little crime, the government began zapping people to get rid of them.

First they made everyone take an IQ test. Everyone who got a lower score was zapped and placed on an island somewhere to be forgotten. Then the government resorted to DNA tests. Anyone who had genetic defects was zapped and placed on their own island as well.

The people of the planet became angry and rebelled. Masses of tiny people banded together and began attacking the giants until, eventually, they were overthrown.

They were able to steal the shrink ray gun and began zapping all of the giants until only tiny humans were left. This solved their overpopulation problem, but then something far worse happened. The tiny humans were no longer on the top of the food chain.

Many humans died in the massacre of chicken run, where a large group of hungry chickens fed on a city of unprotected tiny humans.

Every time it rained, thousands of humans drowned in puddles. Eventually, the only humans left were the ones in the jail and in the city nearby. The mayor of the city decided that in order to survive, they would need to find a way to reverse the effects of the shrink ray gun.

It took many months, but a few men were able to figure out how to reverse the gun by testing it on various objects. One by one, they began zapping humans back into their normal size. Finally, it was Stuart's turn.

Stuart moved to stand on a large X that had been drawn for reference. Stuart crossed his fingers for good luck. Zap! Stuart was back to his normal self. He left the jail excitedly and set out to explore the city he hadn't seen in many years.

In the center of the city, he found a large statue of Jekra, and he cursed at it. He spent the next several days defiling the statue by whatever means he could. Then he had a better idea. Stuart planned to steal the shrink ray gun, reverse it, and shrink the statue of Zekra. He was going to put the statue in a box with some dog poop and ship it to Jekra.

The shrink ray gun was easy to steal. No one seemed to want anything to do with it anymore. Stuart traveled back the statue, thinking about all the jerks he stole from and about how they were probably all dead. He laughed at them and mocked them because he was still alive and they weren't.

Stuart told himself that he was alive because what he did was right and all those jerks were wrong.

When he reached the statue he rotated the dial and then aimed at the life-like statue of the biggest jerk in the history of the universe. He pulled the trigger and nothing happened. Stuart studied the dial again and rotated it a little more.   He aimed at a nearby rock and pulled the trigger. Again, nothing happened. He cursed under his breath, turned the gun around and looked straight down the barrel of the gun. Zap!

Stuart watched as the clouds shot towards him.

"I'm flying!" he thought to himself.

Even though it was mid-day, he could now see the stars. Stuart panicked and wondered how to stop it. He looked down and realized with horror that he was so big, his planet was disappearing beneath him. Then he could not breathe. At first he believed it was because he was terrified, but then he realized it was because his head was in space.

He took in a massive last breath that sucked all of the oxygen off of his planet. He didn't even feel it when his massive weight crushed what was left of his world. Stuart held his breath as long as he could.

He was so big now, that his planet's sun was now a tiny speck of glowing dust headed for his eye. Stuart tried to bat it away but he was still growing. As the star collapsed on itself and slammed into Stuart, a black hole formed. Stuart continued to grow until finally he could no longer hold his breath. Just as his heart stopped beating, the black hole lodged itself in his belly button.

Now you might be feeling sorry for Stuart, and that's ok. Maybe Stuart was a really nice guy and I just told you about some horrible things he did so you wouldn't feel so badly for him. Or maybe he was a jerk and really did deserve it. You may never know. The important thing to remember is that no one in this story will ever know what really happened, because everyone who was there to witness it died. You should be glad I'm telling you so that you don't spend hours wondering what the hell happened. You're welcome.

CHAPTER THIRTY-TWO

Jekra tapped on the holding cell glass to wake Bleek, who had fallen asleep waiting for him. Bleek stirred in his sleep and then slowly remembered where he was. For a moment, he had thought he was back in the holding cell with Shuey.

Jekra had a bag with him. He removed some papers from the bag and held them up to the glass for Bleek to look at.

"The first page is instructions on how to get to your home," Jekra informed him.

"How do you know what planet I'm from?" Bleek asked curiously.

"I had my system scan your DNA. I've been to your home and it's actually quite lovely. Fortunately, it's still around in this reality."

Jekra's good news gave Bleek hope.

"The second page is instructions on how to jump back to the reality you came from. And the third page is directions on how to use the device to explore realities before actually traveling there," Jekra explained. "Now, for the bad news. I have analyzed your A.R.D and it is not built for continual use. I estimate that you have at least one jump left, maybe two, so you're going to have to make a very final decision on what to do."

"How will I know when the device won't work anymore?"

"They usually get left behind in the reality you came from, and they will no longer turn on."

Bleek frowned. "How much time do I have to decide?" he asked worriedly.

"I have a small window of time to get you to the ship tomorrow. You'll have to make your decision before we get to the ship," Jekra warned him. "Oh and I'm going to need your help with something."

"Sure," Bleek agreed.

"I'm going to need to you shift into something small enough to leave in this bag I'm carrying."

Bleek looked closely at the bag and decided that a small rodent would be fine. "Anything else?"

Jekra hesitated.

"If you decide to return to your reality, I would like you to give this journal to your Spee," Jekra told him.

"What's in the journal?" Bleek asked.

"It's a letter I wrote to him," Jekra admitted. "It's only for him though. I'd prefer that no one else reads it."

"And if I decide not to return?"

"Then I'll keep it."

Bleek considered his request thoughtfully. "If I return, I promise to give it to him. And I promise no one else will read it."

Jekra made sure Bleek had more food and left him alone to make his decision. Bleek wished that Shuey were there to talk him through this.

Meanwhile, Spee was still working with Pock to save their planet.

After having to listen to Pock for two days, Spee had almost given up several times. He had considered flying straight into the black hole just to escape the annoying scientist.

Pock was so full of himself.   All of the ideas that had not worked, someone else, and not Pock, had thought of them. Yet all the ideas Pock was sure would work were his -they just needed some "fine tuning," as he would say.

Spee suddenly had a major "aha" moment, but it had nothing to do with saving the planet. Spee realized how similar he and Pock were and it terrified him. Spee realized how hard it must be to love someone like that. He felt sorry for Eep and everyone else he had ever liked. Spee decided that if he ever made it out of this situation, he was going to remedy this.

"Hey Pock," Spee called out. "Do you mind sitting here quietly for a while so I can actually think about solving this problem, instead of fantasizing about ways to stop your incessant and unnecessary communication?"

Pock looked at Spee with shock. The look of shock quickly changed to anger, and then to hurt, but he sat down at a computer and began running simulations quietly.

With Pock no longer looking over his shoulder, Spee returned to the computer that was linked with his ship and tried to send a coded message to Bleek and Shuey. He used the vacuum bot program and embedded a message in the coding.

Shuey and Steph had been watching the computer and surveillance cameras in shifts, waiting for Spee or Bleek to return. Both of them were a mess, not knowing what was going on.

"I'm going to kill him when he comes back," Shuey pouted.

"Spee or Bleek?" Steph asked for clarification.

"Both of them, actually."

Steph sat in front of the computer vigilantly. A vacuum bot entered their hideout. Shuey looked at it with confusion.

"What are you doing in here?" she asked it.

It had no bucket, nor was it vacuuming. It approached her slowly, then ran into the mattress she was sitting on. Then it backed up and ran into the mattress again.

"What's wrong with that thing?" Steph wondered, tilting her head slightly to the right.

"Bleek? Shuey?" the bot said.

"Yes?" Shuey replied to it.

"It's Spee," the bot said as it ran into the mattress a few

more times.

Shuey picked it up and looked into its robot eyes.

"Can you see me?" Shuey asked it.

"No. I have to be quick," Spee explained through the vacuum bot.

"Wait Spee. Bleek is gone."

"What?! Where?!"

"He took the A.R.D," Shuey couldn't say it without crying. "He left a note."

"Why?" Spee asked. Spee felt sick to his stomach. His friend Bleek was gone. "Never mind. You needn't say it. I already know why."

"Come back Spee, we need you," Steph chimed in.

"They're holding me here until we save the planet or die trying," Spee explained.

"What's going on?" Shuey asked.

"Look for yourself."

Shuey carried the bot with her to the computer and they took a look outside.

"What the…" Shuey didn't finish her sentence.

"It's my fault," the bot spoke for Spee. "I'm so sorry guys."

Shuey and Steph looked at each other sadly. They were not sure how to respond, so they didn't.

"You guys get out of here when the other ships leave. I don't want you here when the black hole pulls the planet in," he instructed.

"We can't leave you Spee," Shuey insisted.

"I have to go now. Please promise me you'll save yourselves when the time comes."

"We promise," Steph said for both of them.

The vacuum bot stopped channeling Spee and tried to return to the floor. Shuey set it down and watched it return to its vacuuming.

"Kind of ironic isn't it?" Steph suggested.

"What?"

"Keely always joked that your belly button was a black hole. Wait until she hears about this."

CHAPTER THIRTY-THREE

"Wake up, Jude."

Bleek thought he heard his mom's voice.

"Jude, if you don't get up now, you're going to be late for school and I'm going to be late for work."

Bleek opened his eyes. His mother was looking down at him with a stern face.

"Mom?" Bleek could not believe his eyes.

"UP!" she ordered loudly.

Bleek jumped up off of his bed.

"Mom I'm so sorry I said hurtful things to you," Bleek cried and ran to hug her.

"I forgive you sweetheart, but you still can't go to your friend's party this weekend." She hugged him back.

"Wait," Bleek let go of her, "You mean it hasn't happened yet?"

"The party? No?" she felt his forehead. "Are you feeling alright?"

He wanted to ask her about the nuclear war but he didn't want to scare her in case she didn't know about it yet.

"I think I might still be dreaming." Bleek pinched himself.

"Jude honey, if you're not feeling well, you can stay home," she offered.

"Will you call off work and stay home with me?" Bleek asked hopefully.

"I can't. You know that." She hesitated.

"Will you make me breakfast at least?" Bleek begged her.

"It's already made and waiting for you."

She turned to leave his room.

Bleek ran past her excitedly and galloped down the stairs and into the kitchen. His cat was sitting on one of the empty chairs watching him with lazy eyes.

"Hi Grover!" Bleek greeted the cat.

"Hi Bleek," the cat replied.

"Wait a minute," Bleek stopped to get down on his knees and look at Grover, eye to eye. "I'm definitely dreaming."

"Bingo," Grover said and winked at him.

"Why am I dreaming about this?" Bleek asked.

"You have a big decision to make and your best friend isn't here to help, so I volunteered."

"Um…thanks?" Bleek said it as a question and sighed with relief. He felt himself relax a bit, knowing that it was not real.

"So tell me why you want to go home," Grover requested.

"I feel so alone, and lost, and guilty for what I said to my mom the last time I saw her."

"Oh ok, now I know why we're here in your dream."

Just then, Bleek's mom entered the kitchen and sat down with them.

"Jude you haven't even started eating yet!" She observed.

Bleek looked to Grover for help. Grover only winked back at him.

"Mom, I don't have to go to school today and you don't have to go to work."

"Why of course I have to go to work," she responded, while taking a few bites of the pancakes she had made.

Grover stood up and stretched his back legs as he walked up onto the table. Bleek looked at his mother and waited for her to shoo the cat off the table but she didn't.

"You don't have to go to work. This is just a dream. You're son needs to talk to you," Grover explained to her nonchalantly.

She didn't even bat an eye.

"Oh, why didn't you just say so?" she said, stroking the back of the cat's neck. "Jude, honey, what do you need?"

"You're ok with this?" Bleek asked warily.

"It's just a dream silly, talk to me!"

"Ok. I said some horrible things to you before I went to school and then you died." Bleek said, trying to hold back tears. He felt relieved to be able to talk to her about it. "Everyone died actually, except my class."

"Oh honey. I've done that before. I've said awful things to someone before, and then wished I'd had a chance to take it back or fix it," she admitted to him. "You don't need to worry about that anymore. I knew you didn't mean it. A very cool thing happens when you die. You get to see the big picture. It's kind of hard for me to explain so you'll just have to trust me."

"So you're not mad at me?"

"Not even the slightest bit," she reassured him with a smile. "So what's your other troubles bubbles?"

Bleek grinned at her old saying.

"You're not going to believe me," he says.

"Try me."

Bleek spent the next couple of hours filling his mother in on what had happened to him since he had last seen her. She listened patiently and excitedly to him while he talked, and she clapped for him when he showed her how he could shift into animals.

"So now I have to decide if I'm going to come find you in an alternate reality, or if I'm going to return to our reality and help my friends."

"You just found me in an alternate reality. And you didn't even have to use the device to see me," she revealed to him lovingly.

Bleek absorbed her words like a sponge. He felt her words sink in and they rang true in his gut.

"I have to go back," Bleek realized out loud. "My friends need me, and I want to help them.

"I'm so proud of you!" she said, ruffling his hair.

"Can I have one more hug before I go?" Bleek asked her.

She embraced him tightly before saying one last thing to him. "I love you and the cat has something to say before you wake up."

Bleek looked at her strangely and then at the cat.

"It's a black hole, Bleek," Grover informed him. "Tell Jekra. He can help you."

And then Bleek woke up.

"I didn't even get to eat any pancakes!" he moaned.

Jekra was back and he was about to wake him. He looked puzzled by Bleek's last statement.

"I was dreaming," Bleek chuckled.

Jekra nodded in response. "Have you made a decision?" Jekra asked curiously.

"I'm going back to help Spee, and I need your help. They're fighting a black hole."

"How big is it?"

"Very big."

Jekra cringed.

"None of their scientists have been able to figure out a solution. They were so desperate that they asked Spee to return home," Bleek explained.

Jekra suddenly had an idea and began uploading data onto a storage device from his computer. Bleek watched him patiently, awaiting an explanation. Jekra added the storage device to the bag.

"There is a way to make a temporary tear between two realities with the A.R.D. The black hole would slip through the tear if it is properly placed. I suggest you find a reality in which their planet is already gone. The tear will heal itself minutes after being torn and the black hole will be trapped on the other side if all goes as planned," Jekra explained urgently. "We have to go now though. I don't have much time to get you out of here and you won't have much time to execute your plan once you return."

Jekra opened the holding cell and set the bag on the floor.

Bleek shifted into a hamster and crawled into the bag.
"Are you ready?" Jekra asked him, patting the bag gently.
Bleek squeaked from inside the bag.

CHAPTER THIRTY-FOUR

Jekra carried the bag carefully and tried to remain unnoticed as he headed for the ship. Several of his colleagues greeted him respectfully but they did not stop him to talk. Another colleague named Pock approached him and Jekra cringed.

"I need to talk to you about the human in the lab," Pock rested his right hand on Jekra in an attempt to guide him back to the holding cell.

"What's this about, Pock."

"I heard the boy has the ability to shape shift. If I may, I would like to.." Pock was interrupted by Jekra.

"Can we please discuss this later? I don't have the time right now."

"But…"

"Pock. Not now." Jekra pushed Pock's hand off of his shoulder and turned to walk away from him.

Jekra sensed Pock's anger, but thankfully, his colleague walked away from him. Jekra continued on toward the ship and into less active areas. Eventually, there was no one around and Jekra picked up his pace. He could see the ship and he gently patted the bag.

"Almost there."

"What are you doing over here in this area?" came Pock's voice from behind him. He had followed him. "Aren't you supposed to be working with the human?"

Jekra remained calm. He had been head scientist for many years now and had worked with Pock for almost all of them. He knew that Pock wanted his job.

"Pock, for the last time, we will discuss this later."

"I wonder what the high counsel will think about your

refusal of my help on such an important task," Pock threatened arrogantly.

"Why don't you go tell them right now."

"I think I will," Pock said without moving.

Jekra knew he was bluffing but he just needed him to leave. When it was apparent that he woudln't leave, he opened the door to the small ship and set the bag down inside. He fumbled around in the bag until he found the papers he had put in there, and he began scribbling a note to Bleek on them. He was hoping to show Bleek what he would need to know in order to operate the ship, but it was obvious now that he would not get that chance. Jekra had confidence in Bleek, however, as he did fly the shuttle and operate the A.R.D., so it appeared that Bleek did hold knowledge of the planet's technology.

"Are you really going to just stand there and ignore me?" Pock was growing impatient.

"I'll tell you what Pock. If you let me finish what I'm working on here, I'll take you back to see the human."

"How much longer?"

"Not long," Jekra smirked at his own vague response and finished the instructions, closing the door of the ship behind him when he had finished.

Jekra was not worried about what would happen to him after they found out the human had escaped. He had recorded his communications with Bleek and was going to take them to the high counsel and tell them what he had done. He was sure that they would understand when they found out their planet was in danger in another reality. He secretly wished Bleek luck and left with Pock.

Bleek waddled out of the bag and shifted back into his human form. He paused to check out his surroundings and found the instructions from Jekra on the floor of the ship.

Following the instructions, Bleek started the ship and immediately transitioned it into stealth mode. Bleek watched the ship disappear into thin air in the reflection off of a nearby wall. A series of codes that he entered into the ship's computer opened the bay doors in front of him. Then he expertly guided the ship outside of the mountain complex.

He watched the mountain grow smaller and smaller as the ship flew higher into the sky. The atmosphere grew thin until, finally, he was in space again.

Bleek flew out of range of the planet and hid behind a piece of floating space debris while uncloaking the ship.

"I'm coming home Shuey," he announced, while initiating the suggested sequence on the A.R.D.

The ship did not hum like the shuttle did. It shot forward instead, and suddenly Bleek found himself staring at an enormous human floating in space. Bleek cloaked the ship again and watched for a few minutes as the black hole slowly ate everything around it.

A thought about Shuey and Steph snapped him out of his trance, and he flew around the planet until he found Spee's ship still in orbit. He sighed with relief because he had been worried that they might have left by now. Bleek looked down to find that the A.R.D was still there and working. He couldn't believe his luck today.

Bleek was barely able to fly the ship into Spee's but was again pleasantly surprised by his good fortune.

As he exited stealth mode and landed the ship in the docking bay, Bleek ventured out to find his friends. He ran down one of the corridors and almost bumped into a couple of aliens that were scanning the ship again. His quick reflexes saved the day when he shifted back into a hamster and scurried into a nearby corner for cover. Bleek turned off his translator necklace in case they decided to communicate with each other, giving away his presence.

After sneaking the rest of the way, Bleek found Shuey and Steph in the hideout watching the cameras intently.

"Are you sure you saw him?" Shuey asked hopefully.

"Yes I swear, he almost got caught by the patrol."

"Hey guys," Bleek greeted them, scaring them half to death.

Shuey and Steph recovered quickly and hugged him. Shuey frowned at him in disapproval.

"If you ever do that ever again…" she didn't have to finish her sentence.

"You would not believe where I have been," Bleek finally told them. "I met another version of Spee. I want to tell you all about it, but that will have to wait. I know how to stop the black hole."

"How?" Steph asked.

"There's no time for that. We have to get to Spee now."

"But how?" Shuey looked at him questioningly.

"I have a ship!" Bleek bragged lightheartedly. "Do you guys want to come with me?"

Bleek was sporting a mischievous grin, and there was a twinkle in his eye that dared them to say yes.

"Only if I can wear my ballerina of destruction costume!" Shuey responded excitedly.

"If she gets to wear her costume, I'm wearing mine!" Steph giggled and grabbed her T-Rex costume.

They waited until the aliens headed away from them before they snuck out to find Bleek's new flying machine. Bleek hoped that the patrol would not return to the docking bay first and notice the new ship that had landed.

CHAPTER THIRTY-FIVE

"How do you know where you're going?" Shuey asked Bleek. They had safely made it to his ship without being noticed and were headed toward the surface of the planet.

"I saw the science facility in the alternate reality." Bleek directed the stealthed ship toward the mountain base ahead of them. He hoped to land exactly where he had departed from but when they reached the bay doors, they did not respond to his codes.

"I would have been surprised if that had actually worked," Bleek grinned sheepishly.

"What now?" Steph asked, fidgeting with her dinosaur costume.

"We go in the front door," Bleek said nervously. He had a good idea of how to play this.

"You're kidding, right?" Shuey's eyes were wide with surprise. "I mean I'd love to go in and kick some serious ass, but do we really have a chance?"

"I've got this." Bleek's newfound confidence was displayed on his face. He navigated around the mountain to the large entrance doors that were open, but guarded by several posts. Bleek found a place to set the ship down, and he noticed that the patrols nearby knew that something was going on, they just couldn't see him yet. That was when he uncloaked the ship and sent a message of surrender.

"We come in peace. Please do not fire upon us," Bleek announced to everyone outside. "We are exiting the ship and we are unarmed."

The guards were poised to fire, as the three of them exited the ship. Bleek and Shuey came out first, followed by Steph, who was now wearing her costume. They were stopped at the doors by a patrol and a scientist.

"I wish I could tell these guys apart," Bleek studied the scientist, wondering who he was. He was sure it was not Spee.

"Who are you and where did you get that ship?" the alien demanded arrogantly, revealing his identity to Bleek, who recognized his arrogant voice.

"Pock!" Bleek pretended to greet him like an old friend. "Congratulations on making head scientist, buddy!"

"I don't know you! Do I know you?" Pock was confused and slightly embarrassed. He did not remember ever meeting this human before but now everyone thought they were friends.

Bleek ignored his question. "I need to see Spee immediately."

"I'm afraid that's not possible, human. You see, Spee is a prisoner here and does not get visitor rights." Pock crossed his arms defiantly until another alien appeared behind him in a spiffy looking robe outfit. Suddenly Pock changes his tone. "Why do you need to see Spee?" he asked politely.

Bleek wondered if the robed alien was a counsel member. Shuey quietly observed everything while Steph moved her tiny T-Rex arms around nervously.

"Because I know how to save your planet," Bleek announced. He could hear several audible gasps from all directions.

The robed alien approached him.

"I am Counsel Member Grado. I will escort you to Spee," she informed him without delay. "Walk with me, please."

They walked in silence for most of the way. The guards escorting them kept eying Steph uneasily.

Finally, Grado spoke. "I think my bodyguards are afraid of your pet there." She pointed at the dinosaur.

Bleek chuckled. "I choose my companions carefully."

"I don't want to get my hopes up, but do you actually have

a plan that will work?" She stopped for a moment to look him in the eye.

"It's not fool-proof, but yes. I have a plan that could work."

Grado continued walking into an elevator and they all follow behind her, except for a few guards that would have to wait for the next elevator trip.

When the elevator stopped, they walked down a long hallway into a large room with computers running multiple simulations. Shuey was overwhelmed just looking at all the monitors. Spee looked up at them in surprise when they entered the room together.

"They caught you?" Spee asked with sadness, and a hint of mild defeat.

"They surrendered," Grado told him with a smile. "This one says he has a solution."

Spee looked at Bleek in disbelief. "I thought you left?"

"I did. But I came back, with help from a friend," Bleek said cryptically.

Pock happened to walk into the lab behind them. "If you think I'm going to let an exiled scientist and his human pets take over my lab, you're sadly mistaken." Pock gave Grado his ultimatum, "I refuse to work with these inferior beings."

Grado nodded at him patiently. "Pock, there is a ship leaving for our sister planet in a little while. I would like for you to be on it."

"But you need me!" Pock whined.

"I do. I need you on that ship."

When Pock refused to leave, Grado had some of her guards escort him out.

"I don't believe we have much time. The other counsel members will be on that ship. If your plan does not work, this planet will be gone by tomorrow," she informed the group.

"What about you?" Spee asked with concern.

"I'll be here until the end." Grado showed no remorse for her decision. "This is my home."

"We won't let it come to that." Bleek pulled the papers from Jekra out and showed them to Spee.

"Wh..where did you get these?" Spee read the papers with a troubled look.

Grado gave them space to work and left to take care of other things.

"I got them from Jekra."

Spee's mouth hung open again in disbelief.

"He was the head scientist in the alternate reality I visited," Bleek continued. "I would love to tell you all about it once we've taken care of our problem out there."

Spee nodded.

"The plan needs some fine tuning, but here's what needs to happen." Bleek told him everything Jekra suggested.

Spee listened excitedly. "You're right, it does need fine tuning but I think it might actually work!"

CHAPTER THIRTY-SIX

Spee worked quickly to build a remote for the A.R.D. Bleek helped by finding parts and handing him tools when they were needed. Shuey and Steph returned with another scientist that Grado recommended to help with the launcher that they were going to attach to Bleek's ship. The scientist, Revlin, was a happy-go-lucky kind of alien and did not seem to be the slightest bit worried about the black hole, even though you could now clearly see the massive human in the sky from the ground, in broad daylight. Revlin bustled about here and there, quickly but not rushed, and gathered materials and tools to mount the launcher. Shuey and Steph helped him by pushing the cart with everything on it. Revlin beamed happily at both of them as they followed him, with the heavy cart, back down the hall to the elevator.

"Can I ask you something Revlin?" Shuey's curiosity was getting the best of her.

Revlin nodded.

"How do you guys tell each other apart?"

Revlin giggled. "We have telepathic recognition. If I see one of my friends from a distance, I get a feeling of who it is telepathically."

"That doesn't help me though," Shuey poked him in the arm.

"If you guys save my planet, I'll wear a name tag for you, every day," he grinned happily.

"Are you not scared at all?" Steph asked him curiously.

Revlin tilted his head in retrospect. "You know, they did tell me that I was reset once because I was afraid all the time. Ever since then, I'm hardly ever afraid. Speaking of which, if something terrible happens while I'm working you might want to help me out. My fight or flight response is almost nonexistent."

They finally reached Bleek's ship and Revlin began working right away.

"Um Revlin? Can you work a little faster?" Shuey asked while pointing at the sky.

Revlin looked up. "Oh that?"

For a moment, Shuey thought that Revlin might actually be frightened, but then he grinned and went back to work.

Spee finished the remote and began making calculations and running simulations. He wished he had time to run multiple simulations but he only had enough time for a few. He ran the tests until he got the same scenario twice.

"That will have to be good enough. We don't have time to check it anymore," Spee said worriedly. "Do you remember what you need to do?"

Bleek nodded.

"I wish I could come with you but I don't trust anyone else to manage the timing with the remote."

"I'll be fine," Bleek tried to reassure him. "If it doesn't work, I'll get to see what the inside of a black hole looks like."

Spee handed him a navigation file to upload so that Bleek would not have to worry about direction and position and he could mostly fly on auto pilot.

"Good luck," he wished Bleek.

Bleek reached his ship just as Revlin had finished attaching the launcher. Revlin spent a few moments showing him how to operate the launcher and how to direct it using the navigation and targeting systems. Bleek ran through the instructions he had just been shown to make sure he had gotten everything. Revlin patted him on the back.

"We're coming with you," Shuey said from inside the

ship.

Bleek almost tried to talk them out of it, but then he changed his mind. He decided instead that it would be helpful to have them there, especially if things didn't go as planned.

Revlin waved at them as the ship took off. Bleek guided the ship away from the mountain base and engaged the auto pilot. He waited until they reached a certain altitude to start a timer, just as Spee had suggested.

"The giant human would have to be a dude, wouldn't it?" Shuey joked to Bleek.

"Gross," Steph moaned. "Why'd you make me look?"

Bleek's eyes grew wide and his lips pressed together in a silly grin. "You're just upset that you don't have a giant pair of boobies to check out," he quipped.

The girls both giggled.

Just then the timer went off. Bleek halted their speed and began targeting the launcher at the black hole. As soon as the system locked onto its target, Bleek immediately sent a message to Spee. To Bleek's relief, Spee acknowledged the message.

"Now we just watch and wait," Bleek told the girls.

Below, Spee monitored the tracking device they had planted on the A.R.D. He tapped his finger nervously to time it out, then he pressed on the remote switch. It beeped. Spee messaged Bleek to let him know the A.R.D had been activated.

Bleek and the girls watched as the A.R.D flew towards the black hole. It began to slow down but then the black hole took over and began to pull it in. They felt a tug on Bleek's ship as the black hole began to pull them in also, and they waited nervously until a message from Spee notified them that he had activated the A.R.D. The lights on the device began to glow. They waited eagerly to see what happened next. Nothing happened. Shuey looked at Bleek with worry.

"Wait, I see something," Bleek pointed in the direction of the device. It had disappeared, and in its place was a huge black tear that slowly opened into a gaping hole. It was only visible because the giant human's skin was behind it. Bleek panicked.

"The hole isn't big enough," Bleek said, fumbling to send Spee a message.

Spee sent another one back telling him not to worry about it. It was a lie, but he did not want them to be any more frightened than they were already.

"Hey," Shuey noticed something. "I don't feel like we're being pulled in anymore."

Bleek had noticed this too.

The tear began to widen as it neared the black hole until the human almost disappeared completely.   A few minutes later the human and the black hole were gone. Bleek wanted to make sure they really were gone. He took back control of navigation and maneuvered the ship to the right of the tear but made sure to keep a safe distance.

"Woah," Shuey pointed.

From the side they could see space rock and junk being sucked into the tear. The black hole had crossed into the alternate reality and was pulling debris in along with it. The debris field got smaller and smaller until the tear sealed itself.   The rest of the floating debris flew past where the tear had once been and was heading for the planet.

Bleek messaged Spee urgently. "Incoming debris."

The suspense was almost too great.

"Oh my goodness!" Steph squealed with worry. "Those rocks are huge."

Minutes later, a barrage of torpedo-like weapons hit the rocks, breaking most of them up and even sending debris in the opposite direction. Bleek showed them Spee's latest message.

"Mission accomplished!" He cheered and responded that they were on their way back.

CHAPTER THIRTY-SEVEN

Two years later, Spee was head scientist of his planet's science department. His lab assistant, Shuey, had been working so hard lately on their top projects that he had decided to take a break and help her work on TAV's new chassis. She had designed TAV's new body to resemble a real puppy, complete with faux fur. They had uploaded TAV into one of the lab computers so that she could talk to him whenever she wanted.   TAV was excited about getting a new body.

They worked on the chassis for several hours after work before realizing that they needed to stop, or else they were going to be late for Bleek's graduation.

"But we are almost finished!" Shuey moaned impatiently. "Tomorrow, TAV, I promise!" She looked at Spee with pleading eyes. "Please, Spee, can we finish him tomorrow? I want to take him home with me!"

"Sure," Spee said happily. "I'm going to leave now and go pick up Eep from home. We'll meet you there!"

Shuey skipped excitedly down the hall to one of the other labs to get her girlfriend.

Steph was working as Revlin's lab assistant. They were working on a top secret project and she was not even allowed to tell Shuey about it, even though Shuey begged her for clues on a daily basis. Shuey knocked on the door and waited impatiently. Steph was there shortly and squeezed through a tiny gap in the door so that Shuey could not try and steal a peek.

"Oh come on!" Shuey whined jokingly. "Please?" She looked at Steph with puppy dog eyes.

"No!" Steph laughed. "I can't tell you, for the millionth

time."

"Can't I just say hi to Revlin?"

"Revlin told me to tell you hi on my way out," Steph grinned as Shuey finally gave up. They headed for the exit.

They passed Chancellor Grado on the way out.

"Congrats on your promotion!" the girls told her as they passed. "We'll come talk to you about it later. We're running late for Bleek's graduation."

Grado smiled and nodded.

Steph and Shuey hurried so that they would not miss the next train. They ran to the train station, both of them shifting into cheetahs to make it on time. Several aliens, all wearing name tags, pointed and waved.

Revlin had held true to his word and wore a name tag for the humans. Other aliens, who heard about why he wore it, began wearing them also. The shape shifting humans were now heroic celebrities on their planet. Spee had given Steph the shape shifting ability soon after they had returned, and she was always racing Shuey. Shuey did not mind even though Steph was always winning. Thankfully, they made it to the train in time.

"Hey, see that E.T. over there?" Steph whispered. She didn't have to point. Shuey looked and giggled at the extraterrestrial wearing a homemade ballerina of destruction costume.

Shuey suddenly had a funny thought. "You know, we're the extraterrestrials now," she pointed out.

"Oh good one," Steph said.

They stopped talking as the train went through the section of the city that was hit by the remaining space debris from two years ago. Luckily no one had been hurt because that part of the city had already been evacuated. It was now under construction and new buildings were popping up on a monthly basis.

They finally reached their stop and raced home, in cheetah

form, to their cozy little pod home. Spee tried to build them a huge house but they had insisted on a small one with a large yard for their robot puppy, TAV, to run in when his puppy body was finished.

Spee and Eep waited patiently at the ceremony. They got there early to save seats in the front for themselves and the girls. Eep had started her own engineering company, and she was responsible for designing Shuey and Steph's house for them.   She looked happily at Spee and felt grateful to the humans for being such a great influence on him. He had changed so much, and for the better. The seating in the outdoor area filled up, and Shuey and Steph arrived only minutes before the ceremony began.

Pock was their guest speaker, and even after everything that had happened, he was still an ass. After the speech, the president of the space flight school began announcing the names of all the graduates. They did not get diplomas like they do on Shuey's planet, they got their own ships instead. Each graduate left with their sponsor after their name was called to go see their new ride.

Bleek's ship, that he had gotten from the alternate reality, had gone into a museum after they had returned.   He was promised a better one when he graduated.   Bleek had been a quick study and graduated in half the time. When Bleek's name was called, everyone cheered loudly for the hero who saved their planet.

Spee had the honor of sponsoring Bleek, and he got to show him his new ship. Bleek met up with him eagerly and motioned for Eep and the girls to join them. Spee led his friends to a hangar nearby. He opened the door theatrically. They could hear the last of the graduates names being called in the background. Bleek covered his eyes because Shuey told him it would be more exciting that way.   Spee placed a hand on his shoulder to guide him over to his ship.

"Ok, you can open your eyes now," Spee instructed.

Bleek opened them immediately and could not believe what he was seeing. "That's my ship?" his voice sounded a little higher pitched than normal. "It's huge!"

"Chancellor Grado insisted that you have the best ship," Spee recounted.

"What are you going to do with that thing?" Shuey asked curiously.

"Oh, you know, secret missions and such. Who knows, maybe I'll rescue my own damsel in distress with it."

Steph grinned at him.

The next day, Shuey raced home excitedly with TAV in his newly completed puppy chassis. TAV zipped around the yard excitedly, half running, half hovering.

"No more cooking for you," Shuey giggled at him. "Just running and playing and doing puppy things."

TAV barked excitedly. "Steph is home!"

"Oh my goodness, TAV, look at you!" Steph beamed at him and picked him up. "Why didn't you wait for me, Shuey?"

"I'm so sorry, Steph. I was just so excited about TAV," Shuey apologized even though Steph wasn't bothered by it.

They went inside to make dinner.

Here's a really great place for me to end the story, for now at least. I'll give you a hint though.   A few minutes from now, Steph is going to tell Shuey about what her top-secret project is. A few hours from now, Bleek is leaving on his first mission. And a few days from now, you're going to be wishing you had another Wormboy book to read!

Coming Soon!
Out of Phase

CHAPTER ONE
Exploring Atofin

Rihnlin watched the clock in her father's office nervously. She was supposed to be working on school work, but her father was distracted with his own work, as usual, and hadn't noticed her restlessness. She decided to take a bathroom break as a test. Sliding off of her stool, Rihnlin touched her feet to the hard cement floor as quietly as possible and slipped out the door. Outside the large metal door, she waited quietly for a moment to listen for any movement but she heard nothing.

The corridor was bustling with base employees and no one payed any attention to the thirteen-year-old girl that had just slipped away from her parental supervision. Rihnlin continued down the hallway, ducking undetected around corners until she found herself in front of the kitchen. She poked her head in the door, hoping to find the kitchen empty but Mrs. Cates was already preparing lunch. Rihnlin retreated back into the hallway to come up with a good excuse for the nosy cook. When she felt prepared, she plastered a huge smile on her face and skipped into the kitchen.

"Hi, Rihn!" Mrs. Cates greeted her cheerfully. "Hungry?"

"Yeah, super hungry. My dad is too. We're both working on stuff and I was wondering if I could..."

Rihn didn't have time to finish before Mrs. Cates had

placed a large bag of baked goods in her arms.

"Do not tell your mother I gave you that much sugar," she said, wagging her finger at Rihnlin.

"Score!" Rihnlin shouted excitedly.   "I promise I won't tell her."

Rihnlin hurried back out of the kitchen before Mrs. Cates had a chance to ask her any questions.   The cook had a talent for squeezing information out of Rihnlin effortlessly.

The thirteen-year-old stealthily headed for her family's apartment on base with the baked contraband tucked under her right arm.   Rihnlin entered the apartment cautiously, pausing just inside to listen for her mother, but luckily her mom had already left for work.   Rihn headed straight for her bag that she had packed that morning.   She was so excited and nervous that she thought she might burst. The orphans had finally invited her to go treasure hunting in the ruins, and she hadn't asked for permission to go because she already knew that her parents would have said no.

The ruins were dangerous and the orphans would only go in large groups when they were low on supplies. They had promised to take her if she brought them food, and she knew they would not turn down a large bag of sugary cakes.   She tucked the food into her bag, changed into some old clothes and pulled on her sturdy boots.

Rihnlin slipped back out of the apartment and headed for the edge of the base, hoping that her favorite security guard was at the gate, but he wasn't.   Instead it was Grumpy Grandt.   Rihnlin scrunched her cute freckled face with look of mild detest.   Pulling her backpack over her shoulders, she pulled down on the straps, took a deep breath and headed towards Grumpy Grandt with a great deal of determination.

"And where do you think you're going?" Grumpy Grandt asked, squinting his eyes at her as she approached him.   He did not bother to hide his annoyance with her.

"I just came to say hi," Rihnlin lied when she realized this was going to be harder than she had anticipated. Maybe she should have accepted Antigone's offer to help her out.

"Go away, runt," Grumpy Grandt grunted at her. "I don't have time or patience for your shenanigans today, or any day for that matter."

Rihnlin clenched her hands into fists at her sides and directed her best death glare at the grumpy jerk face standing in her way. She couldn't believe this was the only thing stopping her from going on the adventure of her dreams. She turned away to head back and looked disdainfully at the large forcefield that kept the alien jungle and its inhabitants outside. This planet, Atofin was so different from the one she had grown up on.

Her parents had moved here only a couple of years ago, to work for Overmont Tech and follow their own dreams. Her mom was a laboratory director in a technology lab, developing cutting edge technology. The company often sent expeditions to other planets to reverse engineer alien technology. Rihnlin wasn't sure why they were here though, because Atofin was considered to be far less advanced than her home planet Yaris.

Her father was an archaeologist and he was either off-base at dig sites or holed up in his office studying and cataloging artifacts. His latest obsession was an island several hundred miles away that was covered in mist. The natives had many stories and myths about the island but all of them refused to go there. Every attempt to fly over it was thwarted by strange electrical interference that caused the pilot to divert course. Her father had been organizing a trip there but they had yet to find a guide that could take them there on foot.

Rihnlin stared longingly at the blue-green jungle outside. She was an explorer, like her dad and she was feeling trapped inside the base with no escape.   Then she heard the faint noise of Antigone's stolen hover bike and she turned to witness Grumpy Grandt approach the gate to look for the source of the loud noise that was quickly approaching.   Rihnlin grinned as soon as she saw Antigone appear in the distance.

Grumpy Grandt shook his head at her from behind the gate.   He wasn't planning on opening it and Rihnlin wondered what Antigone was going to do.   The hover bike started to cough and sputter and eventually stopped near the gate.   Antigone looked panicked and hopped off of the bike to check the engine.   Grumpy Grandt chuckled at her bad luck, opened the gate and charged at her full force.

"Oh, the irony," he shouted as he ran towards her. "Looks like that bike knows it's back home."

Rihnlin saw her chance to sneak out and hide in some nearby foliage.

Antigone raced around the bike, looking worried as Grumpy Grandt got closer.   Her tattered and mis-matched clothes were looking way too small on her.   She reached into a pouch on the bike and pulled out a popper gun and grinned wildly as she began to pelt Grandt with large rubber pellets.   Rihnlin tried not to giggle as Antigone nailed Grandt in the crotch with one.   He keeled over and landed on the ground with a loud thud and curled into a ball.

Rihnlin snuck out from behind the bushes and headed off down the road towards the river.   She heard Antigone's hover bike start up without a problem and follow along side her from the road.   When they were out of sight of the base, Rihnlin left the cover of the jungle to greet Antigone, who waited patiently for her.

"Thanks!" Rihnlin smiled up at her adoringly.

"No problem," Antigone grinned back at her and helped her up on the back of the bike. "Your mom is going to kill you when you get back.   You know that, right?"

"Yeah, but it's going to be worth it!"

\#

The hover bike was too noisy for Rihnlin to talk over so she just held on to Antigone's waist and watched the jungle fly by.   The road became mostly dirt but the hover bike glided right over it with no problem, despite the horrible noises it was making.   They rounded a corner and Rihnlin caught a glimpse of the river.   The water sparkled in the sunlight and she saw a boat waiting for them.

Rihnlin felt a little anxious.   She had only met a handful of orphans before but today she would be meeting all of them.   She adjusted her grip around Antigone's waist and accidentally snagged the tattered edge of the orphan's shirt on her wrist computer.   Rihnlin suddenly wondered if she should have brought clothes to trade instead of the baked treats.

Antigone stopped the bike a few feet away from a rotting boat dock and let Rihnlin off before she hid the bike strategically out of sight.   She wore her brown hair pulled back in a ponytail.   The ends of her hair looked like they had been hacked off recently by a blunt blade.   Rihnlin played with a strand of her own white hair self-consciously. She loved the color of Antigone's hair and wished that she didn't have the stark white color that was so different from anyone else she had ever met.   No one else in her family had white hair.

A large group of disheveled orphans gaped at her from the boat and Rihnlin was surprised to discover that Antigone was one of the oldest kids there.

"How old are you, Ant?" she asked her friend quietly.

"I'm not really sure.   Sixteen maybe?" Antigone replied and pulled Rihnlin with her along the more stable part of the dock.   "Your Native is sounding really good.

Have you been practicing?"

"Yes!" Rihnlin said proudly. "My favorite Native security guard has been teaching me new words and phrases."

"Tammer?" Antigone asked, referring to the guard Rihnlin had been practicing with.

Rihnlin nodded.

The wood creaked uneasily beneath them but Antigone didn't seem the slightest bit worried. Rihnlin hopped up onto the boat with minor assistance from Antigone and came face to face with an older redheaded boy.

"This is Skidd." Antigone introduced the redhead boy to Rihnlin. "He's our leader."

Skidd held his arm out and Rihnlin reached out to return the greeting, but then she realized it wasn't a greeting at all.

"Payment please," Skidd requested with a borderline rude tone in his voice.

Rihnlin uncomfortably removed her backpack while the group of orphans watched semi-patiently to see what she had brought them. She slid the bag out and placed it in Skidd's hand while trying to gauge his reaction. Skidd brought the bag closer to his face and poked at the baked goods through the clear plastic bag. He cautiously opened the bag and took a quick whiff of its contents. Skidd couldn't believe what he was smelling and he went in for another long whiff.

"Count these for me, Antigone," Skidd requested, tossing the bag to her.

Antigone held the bag up for a moment. "Eighteen."

"Can you split them in half and make sure everyone gets one? We'll save the rest for later," he instructed before walking over to start the motor.